ROBOT WARS

ROBOT WARS

SIGMUND BROUWER

BOOK THREE
AMBUSH

TYNDALE HOUSE PUBLISHERS, INC.
CAROL STREAM, ILLINOIS

You can contact Sigmund Brouwer through his Web site at
www.coolreading.com or www.whomadethemoon.com.

Visit Tyndale's exciting Web site for kids at www.tyndale.com/kids.

TYNDALE and Tyndale's quill logo are registered trademarks of Tyndale
House Publishers, Inc.

Ambush

Previously published as Mars Diaries *Mission 5: Sole Survivor* and
Mars Diaries *Mission 6: Moon Racer* under ISBNs 0-8423-4308-3 and
0-8423-4309-1.

Ambush first published in 2009.

Designed by Mark Anthony Lane II

Scripture quotations are taken from the *Holy Bible*, New Living Translation,
copyright © 1996, 2004 by Tyndale House Foundation. Used by permission
of Tyndale House Publishers, Inc., Carol Stream, Illinois 60188. All rights
reserved.

For manufacturing information regarding this product, please call
1-800-323-9400.

Library of Congress Cataloging-in-Publication Data

Brouwer, Sigmund, date.
    Ambush / Sigmund Brouwer.
        p. cm. — (Robot wars ; bk. 3)
    "Previously pub. in 2001 in two vols. under titles: Mars Diaries, Mission 5:
Sole Survivor; and Mars Diaries, Mission 6: Moon Racer."—T.p. verso.
    ISBN 978-1-4143-2311-4 (softcover)
    I. Brouwer, Sigmund, date. Mars diaries. Mission 5, Sole survivor.
II. Brouwer, Sigmund, date. Mars diaries. Mission 6, Moon racer.
III. Title.
    PZ7.B79984Am 2009
    [Fic]—dc22   2009016770

Printed in the United States of America

15 14 13 12 11 10
 7   6   5   4   3   2

THIS SERIES IS DEDICATED
IN MEMORY OF MARTYN GODFREY.

*Martyn, you wrote books that reached all of
us kids at heart. You wrote them because you
really cared. We all miss you.*

FROM THE AUTHOR

We live in amazing times! When I first began writing these
Mars journals, not even 40 years after our technology allowed
us to put men on the moon, the concept of robot control was
strictly something I daydreamed about when readers first
met Tyce. Since then, science fiction has been science fact.
Successful experiments have now been performed on monkeys
who are able to use their brains to control robots halfway
around the world!

Suddenly it's not so far-fetched to believe that these
adventures could happen for Tyce. Or for you. Or for your
children.

With that in mind, I hope you enjoy stepping into a
future that could really happen. . . .

SIGMUND BROUWER

JOURNAL ONE

CHAPTER 1

Cave-in!

The wheels of the robot body under my control hummed as the robot sped across the red, packed sands of the flat valley floor toward the hills about five miles from the dome.

Thin Martian wind whistled around me, picking up the grains of sand that the robot wheels sent flying into the air. The sky was butterscotch colored, the sun a perfect circle of blue. Streaks of light blue clouds hung above the distant mountain peaks.

But I wasn't about to spend any time appreciating the beauty of the Martian landscape.

Not with a cave-in ahead and desperate scientists waiting for whatever rescue attempt was possible. Robot bodies don't sweat with fear. But if they did, my own fear would have beaded on the shiny surface of the robot's titanium shell. While I was still in the dome, on a laboratory bed using X-ray waves to direct the robot body, all my thoughts were frantic with terror and worry.

Once before I'd been sent on a rescue mission. A real rescue mission, instead of the usual virtual-reality tests for the robot body that I'd spent years learning to handle as if it were my own body. The first rescue mission had been to search for only one person, lost in the cornfields of the science station's greenhouse.

This time was just as real. And far more frightening.

Two hours earlier, four people in space suits had walked into a cave to take rock samples. They were searching for traces of ancient water activity and fossil bacteria. According to standard field procedure, they'd sent back their activities on real-time video transmissions beamed directly to the dome. An hour later—only 60 minutes ago—the images and their voices had stopped abruptly, thrown into blackness and drowned out by a horrible rumbling that could only be caused by the collapse of the cave's ceiling. Now all that remained to give an indication of their location deep inside the rock were the signals thrown by the GPS in each of their space suits, which bounced sound waves off the twin satellites orbiting Mars.

Four signals then beeped steadily, clustered together where the four people had been buried alive.

If the weight of the rock had not crushed them, they had

about three days to live. That was as long as their oxygen and water tubes would last.

Back at the dome, a rescue team was being assembled. At best, they would be ready in another hour. Which meant anything and everything I could do quickly with the robot might make a crucial difference in the survival rate of those four people trapped by the cave-in.

Most terrifying of all, one of the GPS signals came from the space suit of my best friend, Rawling McTigre, director of the Mars Project.

CHAPTER 2

Fast as my robot body moved toward the site of the cave-in, back in the dome my body was totally motionless in the computer lab room.

As usual, I was on my back on a narrow medical bed in the computer laboratory. I wore a snug jumpsuit in military navy blue. My head was propped on a large pillow so the plug at the bottom of my neck didn't press on the bed. This plug had been spliced into my spine when I was barely more than a baby, so the thousands of microfibers of bioplastic material had grown and intertwined with my nerve endings as my own body had grown. Each microfiber had a core to transmit tiny impulses of electricity out through the plug into another plug linked into an antenna sewn into the jumpsuit. Across the room a receiver transmitted signals between the bodysuit antenna and the robot's computer drive. It worked just like the remote control of a TV, with two differences: Television remotes used infrared and were very limited in distance. This receiver used X-ray waves and had a 100-mile range.

As for handling the robot body, it wasn't much different from the sophisticated virtual-reality computer games that Earth kids had been able to play for decades.

In virtual reality, you put on a surround-sight helmet that gives you a 3-D view of a scene in a computer program. The helmet is wired so when you turn your head, it directs the computer program to shift the scene as if you were there in real life. Sounds come in like real sounds. Because you're wearing a wired jacket and gloves, the arms and hands you see in your surround-sight picture move wherever you move your own arms and hands.

With me, the only difference is that the wiring reaches my brain directly through my spine. And I control a real robot, not one in virtual reality. From all my years of training in a computer simulation program, my mind knows all the muscle moves it takes to handle the virtual-reality controls. Handling the robot is no different, except instead of actually moving my muscles, I *imagine* I'm moving the muscles. My brain sends the proper nerve impulses to the robot, and it moves the way I made the robot move in the virtual-reality computer program.

The robot has heat sensors that detect infrared, so I can

see in total darkness. The video lenses' telescoping is power-ful enough that I can recognize a person's face from five miles away. But I can also zoom in close on something nearby and look at it as if I were using a microscope.

I can amplify hearing and pick up sounds at higher and lower levels than human hearing. The titanium robot has fibers wired into it that let me feel dust falling on it if I want to concentrate on that minute level. It also lets me speak just as if I were using a microphone.

It can't smell or taste, however. But one of the fingers is wired to perform material testing. All I need are a couple of specks of the material, and this finger will heat up, burn the material, and analyze the contents.

It's strong, too. The titanium hands can grip a steel bar and bend it.

And it's fast. Its wheels can move three times faster than any human can sprint.

As I neared the hills at the end of the valley, I hoped everything the robot could do would be enough.

But that hope ended when I saw the tons of dark red rubble that blocked the cave entrance.

CHAPTER 3

"Dad," I said into the robot's microphone, knowing my voice would reach my father in the dome.

"Tyce?"

"I am here," I said, my words drawn out and tinny-sounding through the robot's sound system.

"And?" he asked.

Most of the slope of the rocky hill was dull red, with jumbles of rounded rocks resting where they had been undisturbed for centuries. Directly in front of me, a lopsided heap of rock, twice the height of a man, was a much brighter red. This rock was in a new position, unweathered by the dust storms that covered Mars every spring.

"It does not look good," I answered. "The entrance to the cave is totally blocked." I couldn't help thinking, *Every minute*

AMBUSH

11

that passes is one minute less for Rawling and the other three trapped inside.

"What's your infrared tell you?"

The robot was capable of seeing on infrared wavelengths, which was a really weird way of looking at the world. It could show me temperatures of different objects, so I didn't need light waves.

I switched to infrared. It was minus 50 degrees Fahrenheit, and the side of the hills showed up in my vision as a deep, deep blue. The rubble of the collapsed cave was slightly less blue because some heat had been generated from the kinetic force of the cave-in.

Two incredibly bright pinpoints appeared halfway into the hill, with halos around the pinpoints that went from white to red to orange to blue the farther they were from the pinpoints of heat at the center. To me, it looked like candle flames I'd once seen when testing the infrared spectrum, with the air getting cooler the farther it was from the candle.

I described this to Dad. All I could think of was that the bright heat was the remnant of an explosion. But this expedition hadn't taken explosives.

"Doesn't make sense to me either," Dad said when I finished telling him about it. "What about the important indicator?"

I knew what he meant because we'd talked about it earlier. The important indicator was 98.6 degrees Fahrenheit.

The temperature of a living human. This should show up as orange somewhere in the deep blue of the ice-cold rocks. If the space suits had been ripped by falling rocks, the orange would look like bleeding air.

"Negative," I said. "Looks like the space suits are intact."

"Let's pray that's what it is."

Dad didn't say what I couldn't help but fear. Either the space suits were holding their body heat, or there was too much rock between them and me for any infrared to make it through. If it was the second option, we might never reach them.

"Can you quickly beam me some video?" Dad said. "That will give the rescue team a good idea of the equipment they'll need. Then go climb the hill and try infrared from a different angle."

What I really wanted to do was panic. I wanted to roll forward to the edge of the pile of rock rubble and begin pulling rocks off as fast as I could. I wanted to shout for Rawling.

But I knew we'd all have to work together—and fast— for the scientists to survive. So I adjusted the robot's focus to allow its front video lens to survey the site.

I started with a wide angle, sweeping from the top of the hill. In the background there was a flash of the Martian sky. My video picked up the rocks and the small shadows behind the rocks. I zoomed in closer on the cave-in site, confident the robot's computer drive was translating the images in digital form and relaying them back to the computer at the dome.

Just then Dad's voice came through loudly. "What's going on here?" he asked sternly. I'd never heard him so angry.

"I am sending you a video feed," I said, puzzled. "Is it not clear enough?"

"I demand an explanation for this!" he said as if he hadn't bothered listening to my reply.

Why was he so upset? I was doing exactly what he'd asked. "I'm sorry," I said. "I thought—"

"This is ridiculous," he blurted in my audio. "You can't walk in here with weapons and—"

There was a thud and a low groan.

My audio cut out.

Weapons? Had he been talking to someone in the computer lab? But weapons . . . ?

"Dad!" I shouted. "Dad!"

No answer.

What was happening at the dome? I pictured the computer lab. My body was on the bed, strapped in. I wore a blindfold and headset to keep any noise from distracting me. My wheelchair was beside the bed. If I shouted the mental command to take me away from the robot, I would return to consciousness there in total helplessness, unable to free myself from the straps, unable to see or hear a thing until someone released me. If someone else instead of my dad was now in the lab, armed and willing to do damage . . .

I was just lying there with no way to protect myself.

Yet this robot was too far away from the dome. It would take 20 minutes to get it back and another 10 minutes to make it through the air locks at the dome entrance. Even if I made it back in time to protect my body with the robot, all they would have to do in the lab was disconnect the computer, and the robot would be disabled.

And was I willing to take that long gamble and leave the cave-in with four people buried and in desperate need of help?

"Dad?" I tried again. I hoped this had been my imagination. "Dad? Dad?"

"Knock it off, kid," a strange voice replied.

"Who are you?" I asked. "Where's my dad?" This was totally weird, like being in two places at once and helpless in both. "What's happening there?"

Without warning, it seemed like a bomb exploded in my brain. The red sand of the Martian valley fell away from me as instant and total blackness descended.

CHAPTER 4

I woke with a headache, as if someone had been pounding pieces of glass into my brain. While I was at the cave-in site, one of the goons must have simply clicked the Off switch to bring me back from the robot body.

This, too, had happened once before when I'd been suddenly disconnected from the robot computer. That other time, however, Rawling had been in the computer lab. He'd taken off my headset and blindfold before I woke. Now, though, I was totally cut off from sight and sound. I felt the fabric of the bed against my fingers.

I nearly blurted out the first question that came to me. *Who's there?* I wanted to ask.

Where's my dad? I wanted to continue. *What have you*

AMBUSH

17

done? Get me out of the straps and the blindfold and the headset.

But I resisted all of what I wanted to say.

Helpless as I was, I had only two weapons. The first was surprise. So I didn't move. I waited.

And waited.

And waited.

While I waited, I used my most important weapon. I prayed. With the crises I'd been through lately on Mars— first an oxygen leak; then a techie attacked by unknown creatures; the opening of some strange black boxes; and most recently, the discovery that my virtual-reality Hammerhead torpedo was real—I'd come to believe in God. I had discovered that gave me a lot of unexpected peace, even when things looked really bad.

As they did for me and my dad.

The suspense in my total silence and darkness was horrible. Someone could be standing directly above me with one of the weapons I'd heard my dad mention. Someone could have that weapon pointed at me, finger on the trigger, about to squeeze. Or it could be a knife . . . or . . .

I waited, heartbeat by heartbeat, with my head throbbing in agony.

When it happened, I nearly jerked my body a couple of inches off the bed.

It was a hand on my shoulder. Shaking me.

I managed not to flinch. I pretended I was a rag doll.

The hand shook me again and again and again.

I concentrated on staying relaxed. It wasn't easy. The shaking grew rougher and rougher, until it disconnected my neck plug from the jumpsuit plug. My head hurt so bad from the sudden disconnection from the robot that I wanted to throw up.

When the shaking finally stopped, I felt hands at my head. The headset was jerked from my ears.

"Stupid kid," I heard someone mutter. I knew I'd heard that voice before, but I couldn't remember who it belonged to.

"You can't blame it on him, you idiot," another vaguely familiar voice said. "Jordan warned us there could be brain damage if you shut the program down without giving warning."

Jordan!

Dr. Jordan was a new scientist, just arrived from Earth. He'd designed the Hammerhead space torpedo that I'd refused to test because I believed it would be used as a weapon against Earth. Was Jordan behind this? But how could he be? He'd been locked up for five days, awaiting deportation back to Earth on the next shuttle.

"Well, if the kid's old man had listened to us . . . ," the first voice grumbled.

"It seems you did plenty of damage to the kid. Jordan's going to be mad about that too."

What had they done to Dad? And who were they? I clenched my teeth to keep from yelling.

Fingers plucked at my blindfold. I kept my eyes shut as the slight pressure of it left my cheek and forehead.

The hand shook me again. I played the rag doll. I didn't know if it would help for them to think I was unconscious, but it seemed the best chance I had, no matter how small.

"Help me lift him into the wheelchair," voice one said. "He's out like a clubbed fish."

"I don't want to bring him to Jordan like this, though," voice two answered. "Then we'll have too much to explain."

"We might not have any choice. If the kid's brain circuits are scrambled, he'll never come out of this. Jordan's going to kill us for it."

"If Jordan's going to go nuts on us anyway, what will five minutes hurt?" voice two said.

I strained to place a face with the voice. It came to me. One of the security force. I'd been with him on the platform buggy during the dome's oxygen crisis.

That familiar voice continued. "Give the kid a chance to wake up. What he doesn't know won't hurt him, and he won't be able to say anything about this to Jordan."

"Five minutes, then," voice one said. "We wait any longer—"

"I know. I know. In the meantime, let's drag the kid's old man out of here."

Drag Dad out? What had they done to him?

I heard scuffling. I told myself there was nothing I could do from my wheelchair. I told myself the best thing I could do for Dad was wait for an opportunity to help somehow.

It didn't work. I had to open my eyes.

I peeked and saw the backsides of two large men who were lifting Dad by his arms and shoulders. They hauled him toward the door, with Dad's feet trailing.

It had been the operation to put the plug in my neck that caused damage to my spine. The freedom of being able to control an incredible robot body had cost me the freedom of being able to move the legs of my own body.

I'd learned a long time ago not to feel sorry for myself because of my wheelchair. I'd learned to stop wishing that I could walk like most everyone else. But in this moment, with every nerve telling me to get up and run after the two men and attack them for what they'd done to Dad, I hated my wheelchair all over again.

The door closed behind them.

That left me alone. And totally, totally unsure of what was happening.

CHAPTER 5

Five minutes.

Fortunately I didn't need more than 20 seconds, because it looked like faking unconsciousness had worked. All I needed to do was wait those 20 seconds, go to the door, throw it open, and yell for help.

The area of the Mars Dome was about the same as four of the Earth football fields that I've read about. The main dome covered minidomes—small, dark, plastic huts where each scientist and techie lived in privacy from the others— and experimental labs and open areas where equipment was maintained. The dome was only two stories tall. The main level held the minidomes and laboratories. One level up, a walkway about 10 feet wide circled the inside of the dome walls. Altogether, about 200 people lived beneath the dome.

I knew it would take only one good long yell for nearly everyone to hear me. Probably 50 of them would come running. When they did, not only would I be safe, but they'd see the two goons who were dragging away my dad. Then we'd get to the bottom of this, and I'd be able to work with the robot again on the rescue attempt at the cave-in site.

I counted to 20. Then, to be sure, I counted to 10.

Slowly I rolled forward and opened the door. In front of me were minidomes arranged neatly in lines. I looked down the corridors between them. I stared long and hard, trying to make sense of what I saw.

I shut the door again and rolled back to where I'd been.

Outside the computer lab, more members of the security force were herding dozens and dozens of protesting scientists and techies into groups in the main open area of the dome. Yelling would do me no good. Not when it looked like the security guards each carried a neuron gun.

What was going on? For a project like the Mars Dome, it was necessary to have a police force as protection for everyone. But regular weapons were too dangerous. Not only could stray bullets do serious damage to equipment and the dome, but guns that fired bullets could be stolen and used by the wrong person.

Neuron guns solved both problems. They worked by firing electrical impulses that disabled nerves and neurons. No damage to skin or muscle or bone. Nor would they work for someone who stole one. The guns were linked by satellite beam to the dome's main computer. A security code had to be entered before the guns were operative. Each gun was programmed by fingerprint recognition to a specific member of the security force. Even after a neuron gun was operative, it wouldn't work in the hands of the wrong person.

Except now it looked like everyone in the security force was working together.

But how had they programmed the mainframe computer to operate the guns? Only Rawling had the code, and he was under a cave-in.

I sighed. It wasn't going to do any good to roll out into the corridors and begin asking questions. Worse, I had only a little over four minutes until the security goons returned for me. I forced my mind away from questions and back to what I could do to help Dad and myself.

I wheeled in a tight circle and surveyed the computer room. On the bed, the blindfold and headset lay where the guys had dropped them. Those wouldn't do me any good. On the computer table was a small tool set with tiny screwdrivers and some pliers that a techie had left the day before after doing some maintenance work.

I pushed the wheelchair over, grabbed the tool set, and stuffed it down the back of my jumpsuit.

There were a couple of pens beside a pad of paper. I ripped off some paper, folded it, and stuffed it up one sleeve. I slipped the pens up my other sleeve. I hoped some of these items would come in handy later.

Other than that, the room held only the computer drive, now shut off and disconnected from the remote that sent X-ray information to the robot out on the surface of the planet. I understood why my head hurt so badly. Rawling said it was very, very important that I be the one to take my mind away from the robot controls because the electrical impulses of my brain were so closely intertwined with the computer. When one of the goons clicked the Off switch to bring me back from the robot body, it was like jamming an electric prong into the side of my head.

I kept staring at the computer, knowing there was something I'd be able to do if I were ever left alone for a while. . . .

I reached down and reconnected everything. I powered up the computer again and left it on, grateful that the humming of the hard drive couldn't be heard above the whoosh of the vents that circulated fresh air through the dome.

With the computer on again, all I needed was more time alone. That would give me the chance to reconnect my neck plug, which was still loose from when the guy had shaken me so hard. Then, with the neck plug of my jumpsuit sending information to the remote in this room, and with the remote sending digital information ahead to the robot body, I'd be reconnected to the robot. It was more difficult to keep out distractions without the blindfold and headset, but it was possible. If I could control the robot body, I could get it back into the dome and let it do everything I couldn't do from my wheelchair.

I spun the wheelchair toward the door and positioned it where the security goons had left me. I slumped my head forward and closed my eyes.

And waited for their return.

CHAPTER 6

"Where is it?"

Dr. Jordan had taken a chair and turned it backward.
He sat in it, facing me, barely a foot away. We were in
Rawling's office, where the security men had delivered me
five minutes earlier.

I had faked unconsciousness there too as I listened to
Dr. Jordan yell at them for shutting down the computer program without being sure I had returned from the robot controls. But I still hadn't learned anything about the situation
in the dome.

After he'd finished yelling, Dr. Jordan had pinched
my nose shut and poured water in my mouth until I had no
choice but to gag and fight for air.

When I'd opened my eyes, he smiled and said, "I knew

you were faking it." Then he pulled up the chair and asked the question that made no sense to me.

"Where is what?" I asked in return. Cold water soaked the front of my jumpsuit, but I refused to let him know it made me uncomfortable.

Dr. Jordan nodded at a security guard. He brought over a handheld metal scanner, the type used to search for metal in rocks. The guard flicked it on, and the wand began beeping as he passed it over me.

The search was quick. They found the tool set, pens, and paper and took those. But the metal scanner results evidently weren't enough to satisfy Dr. Jordan. "So, it's not on you. Where is it?"

"Where is what?" I repeated.

"Project 3."

"Project 3?"

"Don't play games with me," he warned.

His face was round like his gold-rimmed glasses, which usually seemed to bounce light so it looked like he had two perfectly circular mirrors in front of his eyes. His goatee was round too, and his nose was turned up at the end, showing the dark of his nostrils as two more circles. From a distance, I'd always thought he looked harmless, like an absentminded clown. Just five days ago, when I'd refused to take the space torpedo on a test flight, however, I'd learned he was anything but harmless. He'd sounded like a military general rather than the scientist I had been led to believe he was. Now, with him looming in front of me, I realized how big he really was. At this angle, without light bouncing off his glasses, I saw into his cold eyes. And I shivered.

"I'm not playing games," I said. "Where's my dad? What's happening in the dome?"

As the security guards had pushed me through the dome, I'd kept my head down like I was unconscious. But I still heard enough commotion and worried voices to know that something terrible was happening.

"I want to know where you have it." Dr. Jordan leaned forward and put his hands on my shoulders. I smelled stale coffee on his breath. He squeezed his fingers into the muscles of my shoulders with such force I almost gasped. "I want to know what Ashley told you about it."

Ashley. His daughter. And my only friend close to my age. Hearing her name stabbed me with pain, and I had to look away.

Everyone knew she'd died on our test mission when she flew Dr. Jordan's space torpedo directly into Phobos, one of the moons of Mars. I wore a silver earring of hers on a chain around my neck. The earring was a small cross. She'd given it to me as a friendship pledge when I'd had to travel far away from the dome to check out the strange black boxes. But Ashley had become more and more secretive about her past, sidestepping any questions I asked. She'd betrayed me by not telling me she was like me—a kid who could control robots through virtual reality.

When she'd chosen to pilot the Hammerhead torpedo, I thought she'd betrayed me again and I'd been angry. But then she'd crashed the torpedo into Phobos, sacrificing herself to save millions on Earth from dying.

After that, I'd had a hard time facing life. She was my friend, and I hadn't trusted her to do the right thing. I'd stayed in my room for two days, not wanting to see anyone.

"Talk to me." Dr. Jordan grabbed my chin and forced me to look into his eyes again. "You have no idea what kind of trouble you just bought yourself."

Obviously he wasn't too upset about Ashley. How could he be so cold about her death? His coldness made me angry. And gave me strength.

"I'm not the one in trouble," I said, clenching my teeth. "You are."

He laughed harshly. "Me?"

"There are four men trapped by a cave-in, and you're keeping me from helping them." I drew a breath. "Something's happening out in the dome, and you're here instead of fixing it. So maybe you're part of that too. Which means if no one is trying to get out to the cave-in and you're to blame, you'll be responsible for those four scientists' lives."

Dr. Jordan's laughter died into a tight, nasty smile. "That's right," he said, lifting a hand from my shoulder and gesturing around the office. "I'd almost forgotten. Your friend Rawling McTigre. He's out there, isn't he?"

As director, Rawling had taken this office over from the previous director, Blaine Steven, who was under arrest because of the oxygen crisis and was about to be shipped back to Earth on the next shuttle. Steven had made his office the biggest single room in the dome. Rawling hadn't yet had time to make any changes. On the walls were framed paintings of Earth scenes like sunsets and mountains. The former director had spent a lot of the government's money to get those luxuries included in cargo. But even a director didn't get bookshelves and real books. Cargo was too expensive. If people wanted books, they read them on DVD-gigarom.

"Not only is *Rawling* out there," I said, getting angrier, "there are three others. If you don't let me go—"

He twisted my arm. "*Nobody* tells me what to do. Not even the president of the World United. Understand? You fall so far below that I could crush you like stepping on a grape." He let that small smile return. "Tell you what. If you don't give me what I want, I'll make sure those four stay so long under all that rock that they become mummies. And I can promise you, your parents will be next to die."

My anger dissolved in instant fear, and my voice cracked. "Tell me what it is you think I have. I can't give it to you unless I know what you're looking for."

Dr. Jordan studied my face. "I almost believe you.

Except you're the only person Ashley would have told. And you're the only person who could use it."

"What?" I asked with desperation. "Just tell me what you want."

Instead of answering, Dr. Jordan stood suddenly. He walked around behind me, too quickly for me to turn in my wheelchair and follow. I felt him grab the back of my jumpsuit. He twisted roughly and yanked hard. The fabric ripped.

When he stood in front of me again, I understood. In his hand was the plug from my jumpsuit, the one that connected my neck plug to the antenna sewn into the clothing.

Dr. Jordan dropped the small plug and patch of fabric into my lap. "There. Now you'll never be able to connect to it. If I don't get it back, at least you won't be able to control it. And if you can't use it, no one can."

It. Did he mean the robot body? Surely he knew it was at the cave-in site. If he wanted it, all he had to do was wait until I'd returned with it.

"Please," I said, "just tell me what it is you think I have and—"

"Lock him up," Dr. Jordan ordered the security guards. "We'll give him the rest of the day to decide whether he wants to help. When he's hungry enough, he'll talk. If not, we'll see if some damage to his parents opens his mouth." He turned sharply and left the office.

As the door opened and closed, I heard commotion out in the dome. What was going on?

One of the security guys took the handles of my wheelchair and began to push.

I didn't know where they intended to lock me up. All I knew was that the neck plug had been ripped from my jumpsuit, and I no longer had any chance of reconnecting to the robot. Which meant I was a prisoner of my wheelchair.

With time running out for Rawling and the other three trapped by the cave-in.

With Dad injured and taken somewhere else.

With Mom in danger if I didn't tell Dr. Jordan what he wanted.

With some sort of takeover happening in the dome.

And with the nearest help the distance from Earth to Mars—50 million miles away.

CHAPTER 7

My new prison was a storage room. Its floor size was twice as big as my wheelchair, and the ceiling hardly higher than I could have reached by standing on top of my wheelchair and jumping with my arms up.

But of course, I could not stand. Or jump.

Nor could I even roll my wheelchair. The security guys had removed the bolts from the wheels. If I turned and moved in any direction, the wheels would fall off.

The guys had also shut off the light above me, leaving me in darkness.

I felt totally helpless. Although I knew God was with me, even in the dark, I felt totally alone. I wished God could talk with me like Ashley had. But sometimes it seemed like I was talking to the ceiling.

I sat in the darkness for a couple of minutes, staring at the crack of light from under the door. My eyes began to adjust to the dimness.

Then I got an idea.

"Hey!" I shouted. "Help! Help!" My voice echoed in the cramped storage room.

Two seconds later the door opened. I blinked against the light that outlined two security guards.

"Shut your mouth, kid," the first guard said. "You're not going anywhere. And no one will be able to help you."

I hadn't really expected help. I'd just wanted to find out how close the guards were, if there were any.

He'd answered my question. Two of them sat right outside the door.

Why was it so important to keep two guards in front of me when I was so helpless to do anything?

I realized this small storage area was familiar. I had stood in front of it barely a week ago with a robot controlled by Ashley. I'd just learned that she, like I, had a spinal implant that allowed her to control a robot through the brain impulses that normally move a body's muscles.

You see, as part of the long-term plan to develop Mars, scientists hoped to use robots, controlled by humans, to explore the planet. Humans need oxygen and water and heat to survive on the surface. Robots don't. But robots can't think or feel like humans.

But what if technology made it possible for your brain to be wired directly into the controls of a robot? Then wouldn't you be able to see, hear, and do everything the robot could?

Well, that's me. Through my spinal implant, I was the first human to be able to control a robot as if it were an extension of the brain.

But not the last.

Ashley had arrived on Mars equipped with the second-generation of human robotics, able to control an even more sophisticated robot. With the portable robot pack, which is a mini-transmitter, she didn't have to be strapped to a medical bed in a computer lab.

The surgeon who had done her operation on Earth had learned from my operation. He didn't make any mistakes that put her in a wheelchair. So she had the best of both worlds. A human body that worked the way it should. And the ability to control robot bodies.

If she was alive.

This room had held the Hammerhead, a prototype space torpedo capable of destroying targets as large as a small moon. The Hammerhead had been designed to be handled the same way I handled the robot. Except instead of handling it with remote X-ray beams, a person needed to be hooked up inside it. I'd only flown it in virtual reality, learning to control its moves in a simulated combat program on a computer.

Ashley had actually flown it once. When she'd headed straight for Phobos, accelerating to thousands of miles per hour before crashing directly into the moon.

The night in front of this storage area, I'd stopped Ashley's robot from destroying the space torpedo because I hadn't known Dr. Jordan's true plans for it.

My heart twisted with sadness and regret as I thought about it. If I'd allowed Ashley to wreck the Hammerhead then, she wouldn't have had to fly it. And if she hadn't had to fly, it wouldn't have taken her into the surface of a moon at a speed fast enough to fuse the moon's rock into a gigantic crater.

But . . .

There was still some hope in my heart.

When I'd woken up yesterday, the fourth day after the crash, I'd been startled. On the seat of my wheelchair was an earring just like the one on a silver chain around my neck. As if someone had placed it there while I slept.

Only Ashley had the matching earring. Or so I thought.

But in the time since, I hadn't seen her. I'd begun to wonder if the earring on my wheelchair was someone's idea of a very mean joke. When the cave-in had occurred, all my thoughts had turned to Rawling and the three others still trapped.

And then . . .

This.

All of this.

In the dimness, I stared at nothing and tried to block out my fear and worry.

And I did the only thing I could do. I prayed again.

CHAPTER 8

"Why do I always have to deal with you?"

The door to the storage area had opened, and a large man filled the doorway. I couldn't see the features of his face because of the shadows behind it, but I definitely knew who it was. In the time I'd had to think in the dark, I'd realized that Dr. Jordan had to be working with someone who used to be high up at the Mars Dome. And because I trusted Rawling, that could be only one person.

Ex-director Blaine Steven.

During the oxygen crisis, I'd disobeyed Steven's direct orders. He'd lost his directorship over mishandling the crisis. Later, when Dad and I and Rawling left the dome for a three-day expedition, Blaine Steven had once again taken over the dome. Only our successful return had stopped him. But now it looked like, once again, he'd been released from his arrest. And that meant he and Dr. Jordan had to be working with some high-level people somewhere on Earth. It looked like those people wanted to use the Mars Project for their own means—to control the Earth—instead of helping to accomplish its original purpose.

Unlike with Dr. Jordan, I knew exactly what Steven meant by his question.

"Shouldn't you be worrying about how to deal with the cave-in instead?" I asked as an answer. "And what about everything else happening in the dome?"

He stepped forward. The two security guys stood behind him. He switched on a light in the storage room.

The room was so small and Steven so close that I could only see his jumpsuit where it stretched over his belly. I tilted my head back to look upward. Mostly what I saw was chin and nose. His face seemed chipped out of a boulder, with thick, wavy gray hair and eyebrows to match.

Blaine Steven knelt down so we were at eye level, like he was a good guy trying to be helpful. But from past experience, I knew better.

"Listen," he said, "it's not good for Dr. Jordan to be this upset. Tell him what he wants, and everything else will go a lot easier."

"Everything else?"

Blaine Steven sighed. "You have a bad habit of asking

questions when you should be giving answers." He ran his hands through his hair and stood again, then stepped out of the storage room and returned with a chair. He sat on it and stared hard at me with his icy blue eyes. If he was trying to scare me, it didn't work.

"Everything else?" I repeated.

"Here it is in short," he said. "Everyone under the dome has been taken hostage."

"Hostage! But—"

"If you want me to explain, learn to listen."

I snapped my mouth shut.

"You probably won't be able to understand because you were born on Mars. You have no idea what it's like on Earth."

I had some idea. I knew our presence on Mars was a long-term plan—taking place over 100 years—to make the entire planet a place for humans to live outside the dome. I knew people on Earth desperately needed the room. Already the planet had too many people on it. If Mars could be made a new colony, then Earth could start shipping people here to live. If not, new wars might begin, and millions and millions of people would die from war or starvation or disease.

I didn't tell Blaine Steven this. He knew it already, and I was determined to listen until he finished.

"Although Earth has been at peace for 20 years because of the World United Federation," Steven continued, "a lot of political things have been happening beneath the surface of this calm. You don't pull together a federation of hundreds of countries and expect it to be perfect. In fact, with some of the bigger countries trying to take more water and resources from the smaller countries, the entire planet has been on the verge of war for the last 10 years."

I knew this. Rawling and I had spent time talking about it.

"Much of the prewar fighting has been done using a very ancient method: spies."

My throat tightened. Rawling had talked about this too.

Blaine Steven smiled. "I'm proud to tell you that I am one of them. I put my country far above the Federation and have secretly served my own government for 20 years, assisted often by contacts high in the military—"

I couldn't help but interrupt. "Like Dr. Jordan."

His smile thinned. "Like Dr. Jordan."

"He's your boss," I said.

"He and I are working together for the same cause. And the time is right to take action. Taking 200 people hostage with only a handful of men is very simple when the only weapons on the planet are in your control."

"But why?"

"We have a number of people on Earth in prison for political crimes against the World United Federation. Roughly 200. Once they are released, everyone here will be released. Rest assured, the media on Earth will give us so much coverage that the World United will have no choice but to give in."

"Four men are dying in a cave-in," I said. "Someone needs to save them."

"But that just adds to the drama," Steven answered with a sly smile. "As does the fact that the shuttle back to Earth has to leave in the next few days or lose the only chance to make the right orbit for another six months."

My throat tightened again. Dad was the pilot. I knew very well how crucial the Mars-Earth shuttle was to our survival. The journey had to be carefully planned so it occurred when Earth and Mars were nearest each other—roughly 50 million miles apart. At any other time, their orbits placed the planets up to double or triple the distance apart.

I protested. "If the shuttle doesn't leave, we'll run short of supplies."

"Exactly. Which just adds more pressure to the World United Federation." He laughed. "Of course, what they don't know is that a select group of the highest military men is planning a takeover anyway." He tapped my shoulder. "And all of us can thank you for it."

"Me?"

"You. The guinea pig. We've been planning this since before you were born. Once you proved how successful the spinal implant could be, we went ahead and perfected the operation on others. You, and what you can do, make for a perfect military weapon. Space torpedoes and remote-controlled robots! Unstoppable."

I closed my eyes briefly. "Wrong. I have to choose to help. And I won't."

"Perhaps," he said, his voice silky. "Or perhaps not. Remember we're holding your parents hostage."

I could think of nothing to say to this.

"There are, of course, the others."

Others. Ashley had had the operation. On the night I'd caught her trying to destroy the Hammerhead, she'd whispered, "There are others. Like us. And we are their only hope." So Ashley was right. But where were the others?

Blaine Steven frowned. I think at himself, not me. "Tyce, let me give you some advice. Tell Dr. Jordan what he wants."

"I probably would," I said, "but I don't know what he's looking for."

He exhaled. "You've always been stubborn. Even as a kid. You'd been walking only a few months when you had the operation that cut into your spinal nerves. After the surgery you spent hours and hours trying to get to your feet again. You refused to accept the fact that your legs wouldn't work for you. You never cried, just kept trying to push up. Again and again. I confess, I felt a lot of sympathy for you."

Steven shook his head in disgust. "Now? Your stubbornness makes me so angry that I'm glad the operation took your legs away from you." He turned and stopped at the doorway. "Whenever you are ready to tell us what we need, just shout. Until then, enjoy your solitude."

The door closed, leaving me in darkness again. But this time it was a darkness of body and soul. What he didn't know was how much his words about my walking and the surgery had hurt.

CHAPTER 9

Some people twiddle their thumbs or tap their fingers when they're bored or nervous or impatient. Me? I juggle. And because I've done it so much, I don't even have to concentrate anymore. Especially with the gravity on Mars being much lower than on Earth.

I always keep my three red juggling balls in a small pouch hanging from the armrest of my wheelchair. So in the darkness I took them out and began to juggle.

I hoped it would keep my mind away from all my fears.

It didn't.

My thoughts kept bouncing around, just like the balls I kept in the air in the darkness.

First, I thought about Rawling and how horrible it must be for him if he was even still alive—trapped, with tons of rock on top, not knowing if he would ever be rescued. I thought about what it would be like for the oxygen in his suit to slowly run out or for him to begin to die of thirst. When I got to that point, I desperately tried to think about something else.

Which led me to worrying about Mom and Dad and the hostage situation. I began to wonder what might happen if the political prisoners on Earth were not released. And I began to fear for all of us even more.

But then I heard my mom's voice in my mind, and I knew what she would say. She was famous for sharing thoughts from the Bible in tough times, and the one that now leaped to my mind was: *"Don't worry about anything; instead, pray about everything. Tell God what you need. . . . Then you will experience God's peace."* It was a verse she'd hammered into my head all my life, even before I'd believed in God. I used to roll my eyes at her. But right now, remembering those words gave me the kind of peace I needed, especially when I felt so desperate.

I started to ask myself questions. Who were the "others" Blaine Steven had mentioned? Had Ashley been one of them? Where were they? And what did Dr. Jordan think I'd taken from him?

Then I remembered Blaine Steven saying he was glad the operation had taken away the use of my legs, and I began feeling sorry for myself. I wondered, for the umpteenth time, how my life would have been different without that operation.

After all, I'm the only person in the entire history of

humankind who's lived only on Mars. Everyone else here came from Earth eight Martian years ago—15 Earth years— as part of the first expedition to set up a colony. The trip took eight months. During this voyage Kristy Wallace, a scientist, and Chase Sanders, a space pilot, fell in love. I was born half a Mars year after their marriage, which now makes me 14 Earth years old. The dome's leaders hadn't planned on any marriages or babies until the colony was better established, so they were shocked when my mom announced she was having me. Because my birth on the planet made dome life so complicated, my mom was forced to make a decision: either send me back to Earth or allow me to undergo an experimental surgery.

Mom knew that a baby couldn't take the g-forces of interplanetary travel and that a trip back to Earth would kill me. So she had no choice but to agree to the surgery.

But just as I was starting to feel the most sorry for myself, I remembered Rawling. At least I wasn't under tons of rock and dying slowly. From there, my thoughts began a big circle all over again.

Finally I decided the best thing I could do was sleep. I let the balls drop one by one and caught them, then put them away.

It was awkward and slow, but I pushed myself out of my wheelchair and curled up on the floor.

Somehow I managed to fall asleep.

CHAPTER 10

I don't know how much time passed until I woke. But when
I did and yawned and stretched, something strange tickled
my fingers.

My best guess was a slip of paper.

Which was very, very odd.

If someone had opened the door to put it there, I know
I would have woken up. Besides, who would have been able
to get past the two guards right out front?

The only two people who had already gotten past the
guards were Dr. Jordan and Blaine Steven. I couldn't imagine
them putting a slip of paper in my hand instead of waking me
up and yelling at me again.

Not only were the *who* and the *how* strange, but so was
the *why*.

The only reason I could think of for anyone to do this was to deliver a message. Of course, if there was a message, maybe then I'd get my answers to all three questions.

Unfortunately reading in the dark is not a specialty of mine. I had learned to juggle a few years ago, I could handle robots and space torpedoes in virtual-reality and real-life situations, and I could whistle Christmas carols very badly, but I couldn't read in the dark.

I crawled forward and pushed my hand toward the crack of light that came under the door. Then I angled the slip of paper and leaned my head as close to it as I could.

I couldn't even see my fingers clearly, let alone any handwriting on a piece of paper.

A solution, however, occurred to me. About the same time I also became aware of another, equally pressing need. I knew about an old Earth saying: "Kill two birds with one stone."

I crawled back to my wheelchair and pulled myself slowly up into a sitting position. I folded the piece of paper and tucked it down the front of my jumpsuit. Then I took a deep breath and yelled, "Hey, out there! Can you open the door?"

Within seconds, the door opened.

"What is it, kid?" the first security guy asked. "Scared of the dark?"

The other security guy laughed.

"Please," I answered them both, "can you put the bolts back on my wheels? I . . . um . . . need to go to the bathroom."

I guessed I'd been held prisoner in the storage room for less than a couple of hours. Still, it felt so good to be out under the dome that I already dreaded being put back into the darkness.

As the security guard pushed me away from the equipment area and past the laboratories toward the minidome living area, I looked around. Up, sideways, forward.

The dome was strangely hushed.

Usually scientists and techies would be walking around in twos or threes, discussing their work or trading gossip. Usually, above me, on the second-story platform that ringed the inside of the dome, somebody would be jogging. And most always, there would be at least one person on the higher telescope platform.

Now, nothing.

"Where is everybody?" I asked, shifting in my wheelchair and trying to see past the legs of the guy pushing me.

He put a big hand on my head and twisted it so I was looking straight ahead again. "No questions," he said. "Eyes forward."

Fear caused an icy lump in my throat. Why did the dome seem so empty? My voice croaked out a question. "Was everybody marched out of the dome?"

I pictured what it would be like for 200 scientists and

techies to be forced outside the dome without space suits. The dome above protected us from a thin, frigid atmosphere of no oxygen and temperatures as low as minus 200 degrees Fahrenheit. People would crumple in seconds and die in minutes. And what if Mom and Dad had . . . ?

"Relax, kid," the security guy said. "Jordan and Steven aren't that stupid. If they killed everybody here, they'd have nothing left to bargain with against the World United."

That made me feel a little better. But not much. Not if the only reason Jordan and Steven let people live was as bargaining tools. What if the bargain didn't work? Would they start killing people then?

We passed through the open space where people usually relaxed in front of fake trees and a little park. Just beyond were the minidomes, clustered in the living area of the main dome.

"Were you in on this from the beginning?" I asked, still looking straight ahead. "When exactly was the beginning? Did Blaine Steven know from the first day he arrived on Mars that he might do this? Did you work for him from the first day? And—"

"You don't listen, do you? I said, no questions."

"Four people are trapped in a cave-in. My dad is hurt. I don't know where my mom is. I need to ask questions. So do you. Like, why aren't you helping?"

"Enough." He said it so angrily that I winced, waiting for him to hit the back of my head.

He didn't. Instead, he turned the wheelchair sharply into the first minidome of the living area.

Except for some decorations and photos from Earth, this minidome was no different from the one I lived in with Mom and Dad. It had two office-bedrooms with a common living space in the middle. In ours, we didn't use the second room as an office because that had become my bedroom. Another door at the back of the living space led to a small bathroom. It wasn't much. From what I've read about Earth homes, our minidome had less space in it than the size of two average bedrooms.

"This is the closest bathroom," the guard growled as he stopped in front of the door. "And be grateful I'm taking you here."

That told me plenty, that the takeover of the dome was so complete it didn't matter whose minidome we entered.

"It won't work," I said. "It's not big enough."

"Huh?"

"The only bathroom I can use in the dome is my own. It was made bigger to fit my wheelchair."

Without a word, he turned my wheelchair and pushed it back out of the minidome. It wasn't difficult to tell he was grumpy about all of this.

Thirty seconds later we reached our minidome. I tried to

block out my sadness and fear. It was so empty without Mom or Dad around. I had a plan and needed to follow it, no matter how little chance it would give Rawling and the others. Time was running out.

"You can close the door, but leave it unlocked," the guard said, stopping in front of our bathroom. "You've got one minute. Anything longer, and I come busting in to make sure you're not trying anything."

"Anything like what?" I asked. "Like running away and leaving my wheelchair behind?"

"One minute," he said. "Those are my orders."

"It's not enough time," I said.

"Make it enough."

"You try living in a wheelchair," I said. "You'll find out why it isn't enough."

He sighed. "Just go. If that's what it takes to make you quiet. Go, go, go."

"One other thing," I said.

"What!"

I pointed at a box in the corner of the dome. It held Flip and Flop, the koala-like animals that Ashley and I had rescued. As usual, they were asleep.

"Can you change their water?" I asked the guard. "When they wake up, they like fresh water in their dish."

"Only if it gets you in and out of here as fast as possible."

I smiled at him. Sweetly.

He didn't smile back.

I wheeled inside. The door shut. I rolled the wheelchair backward so the handles touched the door. I set the brake on my wheelchair. If he tried opening the door, at least I had it blocked.

Although the bathroom was bigger than the others in the dome, it still didn't have much room. Limited resources made it necessary to use all space as efficiently as possible. There was a shower with a sitting bench, a sink with a cabinet under it, and most importantly, a toilet.

Much as I wanted to take the security guy's advice and go, go, go, I reached inside the cabinet. It had shelves for toothpaste, shaving cream, and stuff like that. Beneath the shelves a few towels were stacked neatly.

I grabbed a few sleeping pills, hoping I'd have the chance to use them on the guards. Mom sometimes had migraine headaches and used them when she really needed to get to sleep. I leaned forward and slipped the pills into the top of my socks.

Then I took out the slip of paper and unrolled it. I'd been right. It was a note. But I never would have guessed the message.

> *Tyce,*
> *The only place I could think of is your bathroom. Look under the towels. Midnight tonight. Don't go anywhere. Just wait.*

The note wasn't signed. At least not with a name. The person who'd written it had drawn a tiny cross at the end of the message.

A cross like the one on the chain around my neck.

Ashley?

CHAPTER 11

Not enough time had passed before the storage room door opened again. It made me glad I had decided to wait until later in the night to use what I'd found in the bathroom.

There had been a robot pack under the towels. Like the one Ashley had used to control her robot. Dr. Jordan had ripped the plug out of my jumpsuit, but I didn't need that anymore. I had the robot pack hidden between my back and the wheelchair. Now I just needed to find time to control the robot body, and maybe I could help the hostages.

Midnight tonight. Don't go anywhere. Just wait.

"Take him," Dr. Jordan said, standing outside. Light bounced from his glasses, so I couldn't see his eyes. The rest of his expression was unreadable.

Take me? Where? Did he somehow know what I'd found under the towels in the bathroom of my minidome?

I tried to keep my own face unreadable as the security guy stepped into the storage room and behind my wheelchair.

I made sure I leaned back in the wheelchair, as if I were so tired I didn't care. But that wasn't true. I did care very much. And for the first time all day, I had something to hope for.

The security guy pushed me down the corridor outside the storage room.

The dome above was as dark as the Martian night. On most evenings by this time, I would have gone up to the telescope. Until I'd discovered freedom away from the wheelchair by controlling the robot, the best illusion of freedom I found was gazing into the outer reaches of the solar system and beyond.

"About seven hours have passed," I said to Dr. Jordan's back as the security guy pushed me. "It's not too late to help those people in the cave-in." I had to keep trying. Rawling would if he were in my place.

Dr. Jordan didn't reply. He merely walked at a fast pace.

I could have kept up myself, just using my arms and pushing my wheels. But if I leaned forward, the security guy would have been able to see my lower back and what I had hidden there. So I remained sagged backward against the wheelchair and let them take me.

Soon enough I found out where we were headed.

To the dome entrance.

Where Mom and Dad stood, all alone, trapped in the air lock between the outer and inner doors of the dome.

"It's simple," Dr. Jordan told me, hands behind his back as he stared through the clear, hard, plastic window into the air-lock chamber. "Tell me what I want, and I open the inner door. If not, I open the outer door. . . ."

I fully understood Dr. Jordan's threat. The air lock stuck out of the dome like the tunnels that stuck out of igloos in photographs I'd seen of Earth's far north. The outer door at the end of the tunnel led directly to the surface of Mars. The inner door of the air lock was right in front of us. If someone wanted to go outside, they first opened the inner door and stepped into the air lock in a space suit. With the outer door closed, no oxygen was lost when the inner door opened. Once the inner door was closed, the outer door could be opened. The small amount of air inside the air lock would disappear, turning instantly into a puff of white vapor as the warm, moist, oxygen-filled air made contact with the Martian atmosphere.

But neither Mom nor Dad wore space suits. The only thing keeping them from the brutal cold and lack of oxygen was the outer door. Once it opened, they would live only as long as they could hold their breath.

"You should know from your Hammerhead experience," Dr. Jordan said, "that I'm not bluffing."

As he spoke, Mom and Dad walked toward the clear plastic window where I sat on this side.

Tears blurred my vision of them. Mom, with her short brown hair and concerned smile. Dad, with his square face and dark blond hair.

Mom pressed her fingers hard against the window as if she wanted to touch me. Dad stood beside her, arm around her shoulder. They were both shivering. A large bruise darkened the side of Dad's face.

I reached toward them, pressing the window with my fingers where Mom's hand was.

"Give me what I want!" Dr. Jordan ordered me. "Or you can watch them die."

I didn't remove my eyes from Mom and Dad. "Do they know why you have them in there?" I asked.

"Of course. I gave them a chance first to tell me where you had it hidden. And they were as stubborn as you."

"It's because I don't know what you want. Neither do they." I wiped away a tear and tried to keep my voice from trembling. "Please don't do this."

Dr. Jordan answered by reaching past me to put his hand on the button for the outer air-lock door.

Mom and Dad saw his action. Dad took his hand off Mom's shoulder and put his index finger of one hand across the index finger of his other hand to make the shape of a cross. I knew he was reminding me of all the things we'd talked about whenever I asked him questions about God. Like the conversation we'd had after Ashley died. When he'd told me that there are some things we'll never understand until we can go to heaven and ask God face-to-face. That the important thing was to trust in God.

Dad put his arm around Mom's shoulder again and held her tighter.

"I want your answer in five seconds," Dr. Jordan said. He waited a beat and spoke a single word. "Five."

Mom lifted a hand and pointed at her eye. Then she touched the left side of her chest. Then she pointed at me. Eye. Heart. Me.

"Four," Dr. Jordan said calmly.

I love you. That's what her sign language meant.

"Three."

I quickly touched my eye and my chest above my heart and pointed back at them.

"Two."

"Please don't do this," I said. "Please."

"One."

I grabbed at his hand, but it was like trying to pull away a bar of iron.

He hit the button.

At the far end of the air lock, the door slid open. And a white puff of vapor took away all the air that Mom and Dad could breathe.

CHAPTER 12

Dad pulled Mom toward him, as if he could shield her from the vicious cold vacuum of the Martian atmosphere. He buried his face in her hair.

They were so close that if I could have put my hand through the window, I would have been able to touch both of them. Yet I was helpless to do anything but watch.

I tried to keep my voice as calm as possible. "There is nothing I can tell you," I said to Dr. Jordan. "If there were, I would tell you now."

"I think you are lying to me."

"Put me in the air lock instead of them. It's not their fault I don't know what you want."

Dr. Jordan studied my face.

I lifted my eyes briefly to his, then watched Mom and

Dad again. He clutched her, and her arms held him just as tight. How much longer could they hold their breath? I wondered if it would help to tell Dr. Jordan about the note and tonight's meeting. But that wasn't what he wanted. Still . . .

"What do you want?" I pleaded. "At least give me the chance to answer you." I was ready to throw away the only hope I saw for any of this. The robot pack I'd found under the towels.

Mom and Dad fell to their knees.

Dr. Jordan continued to study my face. "Fine then." He hit the button to close the outer door lock. When it was shut, he opened the inner door lock. Oxygen-filled air from inside the dome whooshed into the air lock.

"Mom!" I shouted. "Dad!"

"Tyce!" Dad croaked.

Dr. Jordan pushed my wheelchair away from the window as Mom and Dad struggled to their feet. "Bring them back in," he told the security guy. "I don't want to waste any hostages. If they die, it will be on video so that all of Earth can see what happens if they don't do as we demand." He began to wheel me away.

I twisted frantically, trying to look back.

"Are you all right?" I heard Dad yell.

"Yes!" I shouted.

"Silence," Dr. Jordan said. "Or I'll put them back in there."

I bit my lower lip to keep from crying. They'd nearly died, yet Dad was concerned about how *I* was doing. It was that kind of sacrificial love that Mom and Dad had for me that had first convinced me there must be a God—and that he did care about me.

Seconds later, we were in the corridor leading back to the storage room. When we reached the storage room that was my prison, the other security guy stood from his chair in front.

Dr. Jordan shook his head and smiled sadly for my benefit. "I could almost admire your stubbornness. It's a pity you aren't one of ours."

One of ours? What did that mean?

Then Dr. Jordan's smile vanished as abruptly as the air had been sucked out of the air lock. "I'm wondering if you outbluffed me. So tomorrow I'm going to put them in the air lock again. But this time I promise I won't let them out alive unless I get what I want from you." Back came the smile.

"Let him out once for a bathroom break," Dr. Jordan said to the security guy. "Just once. That's it until morning. He can brood in the darkness about how his silence is going to kill his parents."

CHAPTER 13

Hours later I was thirsty.

They had left water with me, but I hadn't touched any of
it. With a meeting at midnight, I didn't want to risk the possibility of filling my bladder.

Those hours of thirst gave me plenty of time to think
and wonder in my wheelchair in the silent, dark isolation of
the storage room.

Was Ashley somehow alive? Or was someone setting me
up? If it was someone else, why?

One part of me desperately wanted to believe it was
Ashley. I'd found the silver cross on my wheelchair, and only
she could have left it there, right? Yet I'd seen her fly the
Hammerhead into a moon. I'd seen the explosion, and later
I'd used the dome telescope to see the crater the dome had

named Ashley's Crater. If Ashley was alive, why was she in hiding? And why hadn't she secretly found a way to talk to me in the days since the explosion? Maybe someone else had stolen the silver cross from her before she died, and that someone just wanted me to believe Ashley was somewhere under the dome. But if that was the case, why?

All my hope hung on one single thing: the note. It had been signed with the shape of the cross of Ashley's earring. As if she had really placed it in my hand while I was sleeping. But that would have been impossible. The security guards would have seen her go into the storage room. I would have woken up as the door was opened. So I couldn't believe it was Ashley.

If not Ashley, then who?

It seemed that only Dr. Jordan or Blaine Steven had the authority to direct the security guards. But how could Jordan or Steven have done it without waking me up? Why would either one give me the note? And the robot pack? Was one betraying the other by giving me the robot pack? Or was it just another way to try to get me to tell them what I didn't know?

What was it that Dr. Jordan wanted so badly?

Whatever was happening, I had a lot more to worry about than just myself. Rawling and the other three scientists were hours closer to running out of air. Mom and Dad were among the hostages and would face the air lock again tomorrow if I didn't give Jordan what he wanted. Almost 200 hostages were being used as a bargaining tool in Dr. Jordan's game of war. We were less than two days away from the shuttle launch that was necessary to supply the dome.

Far more important than all of our lives, however, was that the Mars Dome had to survive—for the future of millions and millions of people on Earth. Phase 1 had been to establish the dome, and we were now in Phase 2: growing plants outside the dome so more oxygen could be added to the atmosphere. Eventually people would be able to live on Mars.

That was long-term.

Now it seemed the short term was equally crucial. I knew enough about Earth politics to understand how easily wars started. World War I had begun because one person in a small European country was assassinated. Given the unrest of that time, it had been like a spark set among dry grass, and fighting had spread across Europe from there, dragging in the United States too. Now, with some of the World United countries ready to rebel, a hostage taking on Mars might be all it would take to start another world war. How many would die then?

I was too miserable in my thoughts to even bother juggling.

Mom once told me that it's easier to hear God in quiet times. A nudge in your heart, maybe, or new thoughts that help you deal with your problem.

It was easy to be silent in the storage room.

I prayed, asking God to help. But more importantly

I asked him to help me be as strong as possible, no matter what happened.

Then from the silent darkness around me came a tiny voice, floating near my head. "Tyce," it said from thin air, "listen to me without speaking!"

CHAPTER 14

My head and neck froze, but my eyeballs went side to side and up and down.

"God?" I whispered. "Is that you?"

After all, I *had* been praying to God. But somehow I hadn't expected him to answer. Why would God want to talk to me out of all the people in the universe? On the other hand, maybe the voice was just my imagination. Was I going crazy, locked up in this dark room?

"Quiet!" the tiny, floating voice said quickly. "Don't bring the security guards in here!"

It has to be God, I thought with a quick intake of breath. "But you could stop them so easily that—"

"Quiet, Tyce! Listen! I don't have much time!"

"Okay," I whispered, feeling weird talking to God like this. *Had* I lost my mind?

A much louder voice interrupted. From outside the door. One of the security guys. "Kid, what do you want?"

"Huh?" I asked.

The door opened. It was night, and most of the dome lights had been dimmed. The guard stepped halfway into the storage room, which meant he almost filled it. "What do you want? Is it time for your bathroom break?"

"No," I answered.

"What's going on then?"

"Just talking to myself." Was I just talking to myself? Had I imagined the voice?

"Well, knock it off," the guard grunted, then slammed the door shut.

The silence returned to the darkness. I waited and waited, wondering if I would hear the voice again.

It came. Floating in the air. "See? Told you not to make any noise. Are you ready to listen?"

If it was God speaking, he didn't have to point out that he was always right. But I wasn't going to say it. Not if it would bring the guard back and prove God right again.

"Tyce, take out the robot pack. Set it on the floor."

If I do that and the guard walks in . . .

"Take out the robot pack. Set it on the floor."

I *was* losing my mind.

"There is hardly any time left. Do it!"

Slowly I leaned forward. The robot pack had been digging into my lower back for so long I was grateful to pull it loose. I hesitated, then finally leaned over and set it on the floor. *This is crazy. Really. If the guard walks in and finds it . . .*

I waited for the voice to say something else. It didn't. I couldn't risk speaking again, so I couldn't even ask what was happening.

"Finished," the quiet voice said a few minutes later. "You can take the robot pack again. Don't wait until midnight. Plans have changed. Instead, count to 2,000, then get into the robot body. And don't panic. Remember that. Don't panic at what you see."

Panic? "But—"

"Shhh. I'm gone."

I waited for more.

Nothing came.

I began to count. I stopped counting briefly and did some math. Sixty seconds in a minute. So 2,000 seconds was roughly . . . half an hour.

That's all I needed to wait to find freedom beyond the wheelchair and this dark, cramped storage room.

Finally I finished counting and leaned forward in my wheelchair. With difficulty, I reached behind me and fumbled with the connections until the robot mini-transmitter was securely attached to my neck-plug.

I hoped Ashley was the one who'd left the note and the robot mini-transmitter for me. I hoped she'd be near the robot when I took control of it.

But along with all my other worries, I now had one more.

What was there not to panic about when I finally got into the robot body?

CHAPTER 15

Normally I'd be in the computer lab for any robot control activation. Rawling would insist on a checklist. He'd tell me it was
just like flying, and preparation and safety had to be first.

He'd strap my body to the bed so I wouldn't accidentally
move and break the connection. He'd warn me against any
robot contact with electrical sources. He'd remind me to disengage instantly at the first warning of any damage to the
robot's computer drive since harm to the computer circuits
could spill over to harm my brain. And then he'd blindfold me,
strap my head in position, and soundproof me.

This was different. I'd never used the mini-transmitter
that Ashley did. Good thing it didn't need to connect through
the antenna sewn into my jumpsuit. Dr. Jordan, of course,
had ripped out that plug.

I assumed this mini-transmitter was programmed to her robot, and the controls would be similar to mine.

I assumed, too, that she—or whoever had left the note and mini-transmitter—was waiting near the robot to meet me as soon as I began to control the robot body.

In other words, very, very soon I'd find out who'd left the note and mini-transmitter for me.

I closed my eyes and leaned back. I hit the power button and waited for the familiar sensation of entering the robot computer.

In the darkness and silence and intensity of my concentration, it came.

I began to fall off a high, invisible cliff into a deep, invisible hole.

I kept falling and falling and falling. . . .

I'd expected to see the walls of minidomes, the floors, the roof of the dome. I'd expected to see a person—hopefully Ashley.

Instead, the images sent to my brain were unreal and bizarre.

Two large, dark caves filled my whole vision. Below those caves were two horizontal rows of huge, shiny, white, rectangular rocks. They seemed to be stuck into the face of a weird, smooth mountain.

What scared me the most was that the mountain began

to move. And when the mountain moved, it roared! A hot wind rushed ahead with the roar.

I remembered the warning given to me by the tiny, floating voice: *"Don't panic."*

That warning was the only thing that kept me from screaming in fear.

I watched the mountain move more and told myself that none of this was actually happening to me in the wheelchair, but to a robot body. I told myself the robot body digitally translated the sound waves and the sensation of heat and the pressure of the wind, which my brain retranslated as actual events. I was safe, even if the robot body was not.

It helped. But only a little.

Suddenly the ground beneath shifted and thrust me upward!

Two gleaming balls, white with dark centers, filled my vision.

I couldn't help it. I spun and turned and fled. Right off the edge of a cliff.

I screamed as I fell. My vision became a swirling blur. I knew I had to disconnect before the robot body smashed to pieces and destroyed the computer drive.

But I didn't have time. Just as suddenly the ground appeared beneath me again. I bounced but stayed upright. Before I could relax, the ground moved horizontally, carrying me away from the roaring windy mountain of twin black caves and shiny rocks and monstrous gleaming balls.

When the ground stopped moving, I looked around. The ground was pale, with grooves leading in all directions. A dark, long bridge stretched upward toward the mountain of caves, shiny rocks, and gleaming balls. Each side of the mountain was covered with long, black fabric.

Except now I was far enough away from that mountain to make sense of it. It wasn't a mountain. It was a face. A giant human face. The dark caves were nostrils. The two horizontal rows of shiny rocks were teeth. The monstrous gleaming balls were eyes. The black fabric hanging on each side of the mountain was hair.

That meant . . .

I looked at the ground beneath me and the long bridge stretching up toward the face.

That meant I was sitting on a hand. And the long bridge was an arm. I had run the robot body off the hand, and the hand had caught me and shifted me back away from the face.

Impossible! How could a human be that big? Unless my robot was . . .

I stared for several more seconds, and the face began to make more sense to me. I knew that face.

My voice squeaked, high and tiny, as I spoke a single word. "Ashley?"

CHAPTER 16

Ashley. Not dead but alive.

Very alive.

I stared at her like I was seeing her for the first time. Of course, with her looking so huge to me, I kind of *was* seeing her for the first time.

"Ashley," I said again, still in shock. To me, my voice sounded like it did during the terrible months when it broke into a high pitch when I least expected it. "You *weren't* in the Hammerhead! How did you get out?"

She opened her mouth. Again I was hit with a loud roar.

This time, however, I knew what it was. Ashley's voice. I made an adjustment, and the roar dropped in volume.

". . . tell you about that later," she whispered. "We don't

have much time. With all the hostages together in one spot, they're using infrared detectors to search the dome."

Infrared detectors. Looking for body heat. With 200 people wandering around the dome, it would have been impossible to spot her. But now . . .

"Move to the power plant," I squeaked. "It throws so much heat you'll never be seen against the backdrop."

"Tyce," she said patiently, "I *am* hidden near the power plant."

I looked around, trying to make sense of my surroundings. But I couldn't. Sitting on the palm of Ashley's hand, everything was so gigantic to me that it was totally distorted.

I took a moment to appreciate what it meant to control a robot this tiny. I glanced down at the robot's legs and arms and hands. All of it looked identical to a full-size robot. I wiggled its fingers, spun a quick circle. It worked the same too. The only difference was its size.

"Wow," I said to Ashley.

"Wow?"

"This is a great robot!"

"Should be," she said with a tight smile. "It only cost about 15 billion dollars to develop. You're the size of an ant right now. In fact, that's what it's called. An ant-bot."

I had plenty of questions for her. How did she know about the development costs? How had she gotten control of the ant-bot? How did she know they were using infrared to search for her? How had she survived the crash of the Hammerhead space torpedo? And how had she arrived back on Mars?

"Look," Ashley said. "On Earth, the scientists see unlimited uses for people like you and me. Once we've learned the controls of a robot, we can handle just about any machine designed on the same principles. Aircraft, submarines, space torpedoes, ant-bots. Basically, it's like being able to use human brains to control equipment by remote control."

"An ant-bot, though. What good is that?"

"Are you kidding?" she said. "Medical procedures. Think of how easily an ant-bot could do small-scale surgery. Computer repair. Anything that's too delicate for human fingers, the ant-bot does no problem." She frowned. "But that's not why Dr. Jordan wanted it designed. He's just interested in robots as weapons."

Yes. The Hammerhead space torpedo.

Her tomboyish grin finally appeared. "What's great is that I've been using it against him. I've been able to do a lot of spying. That's how I know he thinks I'm still alive and is going to search with infrared. That's how I was able to get past the security guys who were guarding you in front of the storage room. And later when I talked to you it was because I had sneaked past the guards in the ant-bot to get into the room where you were prisoner."

It was very weird, sitting on the palm of her hand and listening to her speak.

"At first, Tyce, when I used the ant-bot to get you the note, I thought it would be better to let you get into my big robot. But this afternoon Dr. Jordan locked it away. You wouldn't have been able to get out. So I risked talking to you and reprogrammed your mini-transmitter to activate this robot. I needed to be able to speak to you, and I couldn't while you were being held prisoner."

In that minute I decided I was never going to tell her I'd thought she was the voice of God. I could figure it out now, at least. She'd hidden herself near the dome's power plant, then used her own mini-transmitter to control the ant-bot. She'd raced in the ant-bot to the storage room where I was hidden and told me to set the mini-transmitter on the floor. Then she'd done the reprogramming so I'd wake up in the ant-bot instead of the regular robot. That's when she gave me the new instructions to wait 2,000 seconds—the half hour it took her to get the ant-bot back here to the power plant. Once the ant-bot was close to her again, she'd ended the control, lifted the ant-bot onto her palm, and waited for me to begin controlling it.

"I'm impressed," I said, "that you knew where to hide the mini-transmitter for me."

"You're my best friend," Ashley said. "How many times have I waited for you to go all the way across the dome instead of using the nearest bathroom? It was easy for me to guess that you'd eventually get there."

My ant-bot face was not capable of smiling, but inside,

I had the world's biggest grin. *Best friend. I like the sound of that.*

"So if we don't have much time," I said, "what are we going to do?"

"I've done my count," she said. "Altogether, there're only six security guards. That's all they need, because the guards have weapons and the scientists and techies don't. If we can get both our robots working together, we might have a chance to fight the guards."

"Robots working together?" I said. "How? Your robot's locked up."

"Easy," Ashley said. "Get your robot to unlock it."

"My robot is 10 miles away." I paused, thinking of the cave-in. It looked like the only hope of rescue was in first stopping Dr. Jordan and Blaine Steven. "I can get it here in 20 minutes, but I'll still need to get it inside the dome. Someone would notice for sure."

She nodded. "I've thought of that. If we can get the hostages to create a distraction, we'll use it to bring your robot through the air lock."

"Big *if*," I said. I was finally getting used to my squeaky voice. "All the hostages have got to know exactly when to start a distraction. How do you do that?"

"The hostages are gathered in the meeting room. Easier to guard them that way. We sneak the ant-bot in and tell one or two. They'll tell the rest."

Although it was a great idea, I nearly laughed. When the ant-bot crawled onto their shoulders, how many of *them* would think the voice of God was whispering in their ears? "So, you and I just need to figure out the timing on all this."

"Yes," Ashley said. "And soon. Dr. Jordan has sent a message to the World United. If the prisoners on Earth aren't freed within another hour, Dr. Jordan is going to execute a scientist here under the dome. He's going to send live video coverage of the execution by satellite feed, so the media will get it and broadcast it across Earth."

"What!"

"And Dr. Jordan says he'll execute someone else every half hour after that until the Earth prisoners are freed. He believes public pressure will make the Federation do what he wants."

"Tell me," I said. "Please tell me Dr. Jordan is not your father."

Ashley took a deep breath. "No. And that's a whole other story. There're 24 of us, not including you."

"Twenty-four. On Mars?"

"No. I was the one they picked to send here. I was supposed to help Dr. Jordan. Because they didn't think you'd help once you knew what they wanted."

"They?"

"I don't have enough time to tell you everything right now. Dr. Jordan is not a scientist. He's high up in the military and part of a secret group of men with power and money and military control. They're the ones who set up the experiments on the 24 of us. They want to overthrow the World United and—" She stopped.

Without warning, my world turned black and swirled and shifted again.

It took me a second to figure it out. She had closed her hand around the ant-bot, then moved her hand quickly.

But why?

An instant later, from the darkness inside her closed hand, I understood.

"Dr. Jordan!" Ashley said. "How did you—?"

"You foolish, foolish girl!" Dr. Jordan hissed. "I'm going to make you pay for all the grief you've caused me."

CHAPTER 17

I pushed ahead, bumping into the solidness of Ashley's fingers. A crack of light gave me guidance, because she wasn't pressing her hand together very hard. I buzzed toward that crack of light.

"I knew we'd find you eventually," Dr. Jordan said. "The dome isn't big enough for you to hide forever."

There wasn't enough room to squeeze through her fingers. I reached out and jabbed as hard as I could. Her fingers opened slightly, and I burst through. Her hand was cupped, and I was able to make progress up the inside of her wrist.

"It's not right, what you're doing to the scientists and techies." This was Ashley's voice. "Your fight is on Earth, not here."

The fabric of Ashley's jumpsuit loomed in front of me

like an ocean of blue. I grabbed it and pushed up, then slid underneath, letting the fabric of her sleeve drop.

"My fight is anywhere it takes to win." Hidden as I was, Dr. Jordan's voice still reached me clearly. "You of all people should know that."

"I don't believe in your fight anymore."

"Obviously," he answered. "But the rest do. And they are all I need."

The rest. He must mean the others that Ashley told me about. What was it they believed and she didn't?

"Tell me," Dr. Jordan said in a silky voice. "What exactly was it that made you so soft?"

"I'm not soft," she said after a pause. "I can finally see the difference between right and wrong."

"It was that stupid space pilot and his talk about faith and God, wasn't it? I knew I should have kept you in solitude all the way from Earth to here. Ever since then you've been acting like you've heard the voice of God or something."

Stupid space pilot. Earth to here. That was my dad. I'd never known before that it was my dad who'd had such an impact on Ashley. Neither of them had talked about it.

"No matter," Dr. Jordan continued. "All's well that ends well. And you're back under my control again."

"No. You can brainwash a person only once."

There was a loud slapping sound. Ashley drew in a sharp breath but didn't cry. Did he just hit her? If so, it made me so mad that I wanted to run up Dr. Jordan's face and yank out all his nose hairs. But if he found the ant-bot . . .

"You think you are so smart," Dr. Jordan said. "But when the ant-bot disappeared, I knew it had to be you or that wheelchair kid. And when I got reports about stolen food . . . I finally decided it had to be you. Somehow alive. Especially with the other kid unable to tell me a thing about the ant-bot. Now open your hand, and show me what's inside."

Everything for me swayed as Ashley lifted her hand. I was glad to be tucked under the fabric of her jumpsuit sleeve.

"Turn around," Dr. Jordan barked. "I said, turn around!"

More swaying movement.

Ashley yelped.

"The transmitter!" Dr. Jordan said. He must have ripped it from her neck-plug. "I thought as much. Which tells me you *have* been using the ant-bot. So where is it?"

Silence.

"Where is it?" It sounded like Dr. Jordan had his teeth gritted.

Silence.

"I could cheerfully put you on the surface and watch the air get sucked out of you," he said. "That space torpedo was one of a kind. Now the ant-bot. Together that's about 30 billion dollars' worth of science. Just because suddenly you decide you have a conscience. Now tell me where it is!"

More silence.

Without warning, everything shifted violently. It felt like I was in the center of a massive earthquake.

I heard Ashley gasp. Dr. Jordan was shaking her.

"Where is it?" he shouted, losing control of any calm in his voice. "What have you done with it?"

Ashley said nothing.

Just as suddenly, the earthquake stopped.

"We're going to my office," he snarled. "If it's on you anywhere, my scanner will find it. And if it's not there, I'll find a way to make you talk."

CHAPTER 18

From the ant-bot's perspective, it was a strange, strange world.

The walk from the power plant to Dr. Jordan's office wasn't a walk for me. I was a hitchhiker, hidden beneath Ashley's wristband. It felt like I was on the end of a giant pendulum, slowly swinging back and forth with the movement of her arm. Every few seconds I'd jab her skin as hard as I could, hoping she'd feel it and know I was still with her.

"Let go of my arm!" she told Dr. Jordan.

"Not likely," he said. "Don't waste your breath."

Dr. Jordan might have thought she'd wasted her breath, but I knew it was Ashley's way of telling me what was happening.

Neither of them spoke for a while after that.

This late at night, even if the scientists and techies

weren't being held hostage in the meeting room, the dome was usually very still. The fabric of Ashley's jumpsuit muffled whatever other sounds were there, like the fans and the hum of the dome's power plant.

Altogether it was a weird experience.

I might have enjoyed it, but I was desperately thinking of what to do once we got to Dr. Jordan's office.

The first thing, obviously, was to get away from Ashley. All Dr. Jordan needed to do was sweep a scanner in the air within a couple of feet of Ashley, and it would give him a *beep-beep-beep* confirmation of the ant-bot's location.

But how could I get away?

The jump would certainly smash the ant-bot. After all, it would be no different than taking my regular-size robot body and leaping off a cliff over half a mile high.

I doubted I'd be able to crawl up her arm and then down her entire body to the floor in enough time.

So I'd have to depend on Ashley. Which was why I kept jabbing her wrist to remind her exactly where I was.

I shouldn't have worried for even a second.

As soon as Dr. Jordan pushed her into his office, she hit the light switch. The diffused, bluish light that made it through the fabric of her jumpsuit became totally black.

"Let go!" she shouted. "Let go!"

Again my world became swirling, rocking, confusing.

I had a sensation of falling, which stopped instantly a heart-beat later. What was happening?

"You tripped me!" Ashley shouted. "I think I broke my wrist when it hit the floor."

She means that for me. To let me know the floor is nearby.

"Get up, you stupid girl."

I propelled the ant-bot forward and fell again, very briefly. *Floor!*

It was still dark. I didn't know what direction I was headed, but I moved as fast as the tiny robot wheels would let me.

Seconds later the light snapped on again.

My video lens caught movement, and instinctively I spun hard right.

Something gigantic came down, thudding to the floor with vibrations that wobbled me. A short gust of air blew me forward.

I'd just missed being squashed by Dr. Jordan's foot! It would have destroyed the ant-bot's computer without warning and probably scrambled my own brain circuits.

I wheeled as hard as I could toward the nearest wall, which seemed like a vertical cliff miles high. When I reached the base, I found plenty of room beneath the baseboard to hide.

I waited.

"Please don't tape my wrists to this chair," Ashley said.

"Shut your mouth. No amount of begging will stop me."

Again, Ashley was trying to help me by letting me know what was happening. She was one gutsy girl.

She and Dr. Jordan were in the center of the room. But what could I do to help?

"Hey," Ashley said, "why is the satellite feed hooked up to your computer? Isn't that supposed to be in the director's office?"

"You have too many questions."

"Does this mean you're the only one who can contact Earth?" she asked. "That's the only satellite feed under the dome, isn't it?"

"Silence!" Dr. Jordan barked.

Ashley knew Dr. Jordan would get mad. So why had she talked about the satellite feed twice?

I answered my own question by remembering what she'd told me earlier. *"If the prisoners on Earth aren't freed within another hour, Dr. Jordan is going to execute a scientist here under the dome. He's going to send live video coverage of the execution by satellite feed, so the media will get it and broadcast it across Earth. . . . He believes public pressure will make the Federation do what he wants."*

One hour left before the first execution.

Ashley was trying to tell me that the only way of reaching Earth was through the satellite feed here in this office.

Which meant if I could destroy the satellite feed, Dr. Jordan would have to wait before executing anyone.

But that was a big, big *if* for a small, small ant-bot. . . .

CHAPTER 19

I followed the base of the wall at full speed, reached a corner, and kept going as fast as I could in the new direction.

In a full-size body, it would have taken only three steps to reach the desk on the other side of Dr. Jordan's office. In the ant-bot, it seemed like half a mile. By the time I completed the journey, Dr. Jordan had returned with the scanner to search Ashley.

Although from my perspective it was too far to see into the middle of the room, I knew the scanner was not much different from the metal detector wands I'd seen in movies.

"After this," I heard Ashley ask, "what next? How do you get back to Earth? How do you know you won't be arrested?"

Computer cables hung from the desk, falling in loose coils on the floor. To me the cables looked like massive tree trunks, with the surface rough enough for me to climb them. So I reached up with one of the ant-bot's tiny arms and began climbing.

"How are you going to get away with this?" Ashley persisted. "I thought you were much smarter."

Arm over arm, I pulled myself upward. Rawling had once trained me for this in my regular-size robot.

I guessed Ashley was asking Dr. Jordan questions to distract him. She didn't know what I was doing, but I'm sure she wanted to delay him.

"I mean," she continued, "you can't stay on Mars forever. And you'll be arrested as soon as you step off the shuttle."

I kept climbing. I didn't expect Dr. Jordan to respond.

But he did. I guessed he was probably too vain to want a girl Ashley's age to think he was stupid.

"There's plenty of places I can hide on the Moon-base," he said. "And that's where the shuttle will make an unexpected stop. From the moon, I can take any number of daily flights back down to Earth."

The Moon-base, I thought. It had been established 10 years before the Mars Project. With short shuttles making it easy to deliver supplies and work parties, it now covered the size of a city, while the base on Mars was still little more than the original dome.

I heard the *beep-beep-beep* of the scanner. I was three-quarters of the way up the cable.

"Aha," Dr. Jordan said. "Hidden in your hair!"

"That's a hair clip," Ashley said. "I can save you the trouble. I don't have the ant-bot."

"Nice try," he replied.

I reached the top of the cable. The ant-bot wasn't tired, of course, because robots never tire. They run until the power pack is depleted. I hoped that either a robot this small was very efficient or that Ashley had charged the power pack recently.

"Told you," Ashley said. "Hair clip."

That let me imagine the scene in the center of the room. If her arms were taped to the armrest of a chair, Dr. Jordan would be leaning over her, disappointed to find only a hair clip.

I scurried across the desk in the shadow of the computer. It was like walking along the bottom of a massive building.

The scanner beeped again.

"Another hair clip," Ashley said.

I ran beneath the shell of the computer. It was much dimmer, but I could look up and get enough light through the tiny cooling vents. There was a gap in the underside of the computer shell. It would allow me to climb into the computer, except the underside was too high for me to reach. Like a person standing beneath a ceiling.

And even if I got in there, what could I do to short-circuit it?

That's when I realized I had asked exactly the right question.

Short-circuit.

Safely hidden, I surveyed the top of Dr. Jordan's desk.
There was a pen, looking like a log to me. And a paper clip.

The pen was almost right beside the computer. I scam-
pered out and pushed one end. I felt very much like an ant
as half of the pen slowly rolled beneath the computer.

"How do you know that someone else didn't take the
ant-bot?" Ashley asked from the center of the room, her voice
echoing weirdly. "Because I can tell you that I don't have it."

"No one else but you or the wheelchair kid can use it."

"What if someone decided to use it as proof of the existence of your secret military program? What if the right people
on Earth somehow found out that you've taken billions and
billions from government programs?"

I heard the sound of a slap.

"Is that what you do when you don't have a good answer?"
Ashley asked. "Hit people? Like that proves you right?"

Ashley could only be doing this to distract him. Maybe
she'd seen over his shoulder and noticed my little movements
on the desk. If that was true, I didn't have much time. I scrambled back from the edge of the bottom of the computer and
went for the paper clip. I wrestled with it and managed to drag
it under the computer.

"Tell me where you've hidden Project 3," Dr. Jordan hissed.

I lifted the paper clip, balancing it on end. Twice it nearly
fell. But I managed to push it up into the gap. It leaned against

the edge of the gap, and I was able to climb onto the pen. One big shove and the paper clip fell into the base of the computer.

"There's nothing you can do to me," Ashley said with determined defiance.

"Really?" Dr. Jordan asked.

With one hand I was able to grab the edge of the gap and pull myself up. With the other hand I pushed and let the ant-bot topple inside. I was now in the guts of the computer, armed with a paper clip.

I froze as I heard Dr. Jordan's next words.

"Fine," he said to Ashley. "You'll talk when I bring the wheelchair kid in here and show you how painful I can make life for him."

"Tyce? How can you hurt Tyce?"

I frantically wrestled the paper clip.

"Very easily. See you in a minute." He laughed cruelly. "Sit tight while I'm gone."

I heard the door shut behind him.

"Tyce?" Ashley called out frantically a few seconds later. "Did you hear that? You need to leave the ant-bot!"

I was too busy with the paper clip to answer.

CHAPTER 20

I opened my eyes in the darkness of the storage room.

How long before Dr. Jordan arrives from his office on the other side of the dome?

I didn't waste any time. First I reached behind me and disconnected the transmitter from my neck. I dropped it down the back of my jumpsuit again. All I could do was hope Dr. Jordan didn't decide to search me again. But there was no point in trying to dump it. Without the transmitter, Ashley and I had no chance at all.

Seconds later the door opened without warning. It was Dr. Jordan. With the security guard beside him.

"Take him," Dr. Jordan commanded. "And follow me to my office."

"It's very simple, Ashley." Dr. Jordan paced back and forth in front of both of us. He had taken me into his office and sent the security guard back to help watch the other hostages. Ashley was still in her chair, taped by the arms to the arm-rests. I was in my wheelchair, helpless as always. "You tell me where you've hidden Project 3, or your friend Tyce becomes the first hostage to be executed."

Dr. Jordan pointed at the satellite feed attached to his computer. "It will make for a spectacular news story—don't you think? People will be riveted to their 3-D sets for television his-tory. He's young, he's in a wheelchair, and not only was he the first person born on Mars, he'll be the first to die on Mars."

Ashley turned her head and stared at me. Her face twisted with horror and dread.

"No," I said. "You can't tell him."

"Best of all, Ashley," Dr. Jordan continued, "you'll be right here watching it live."

Dr. Jordan moved to his desk and picked up a neuron gun. He pointed it at my wrist, which rested on the armrest of my wheelchair.

Then he smiled and squeezed the trigger.

There was no sound, nothing for the eye to see. But the electrical impulses hit me instantly, disabling the nerve end-ings of my left wrist and hand.

I couldn't help myself. I lifted my other arm and yelled. My left hand and wrist hung uselessly.

"How was that?" Dr. Jordan asked Ashley. "Would you like to see more?"

"Please don't shoot him again," I heard Ashley beg above the pain that seemed to roar in my ears. "Project 3 is in the top drawer of your desk."

I lifted my head as if it had been jerked by a puppet string. I stared at her in shock that she'd told him. The last thing I'd done with the ant-bot before waking in my own body was scurry from the computer to the edge of the desk and drop in that drawer. Was she betraying me again?

"You're lying to me," Dr. Jordan told her.

"No, I'm not. Your own office is the last place in the world you'd look."

Slowly Dr. Jordan moved to his desk. He opened the drawer and bent over to see better. A second later he plucked something out and balanced it on his palm. He looked at it against the light. "It really *is* the ant-bot," he said, grinning. "Clever. Very clever. Too bad you didn't remain one of us."

"You've got what you want," Ashley said. "At least let us join his mom and dad now."

Dr. Jordan's grin widened. "Hardly. It's time for Tyce's execution. And if they don't release the prisoners on Earth, a half hour later you'll follow. After all, why waste good scientists and techies when I can get rid of the two who have made my life the most miserable over the past week?"

"No!" Ashley shouted. "I told you where to find what you wanted. You have to—" She stopped shouting as Dr. Jordan pointed the neuron gun at her.

"That's better. Noise gives me such a headache." Before facing the computer and satellite feed, he spoke to me one more time. "Time to make you a television star. It will be a performance to die for."

CHAPTER 21

Normally the person contacting Earth sat in a chair in front of the satellite feed, a simple black box with a small video lens.

But Dr. Jordan shoved the chair aside, returned for me, and pushed my wheelchair forward until I was a couple of feet away, staring directly into the eye of the camera.

"This will be so simple," he said. "You're a sitting duck. Perfect height to catch all the expressions on your face."

"I feel sorry for you," I said.

It caught him off guard. "*You* feel sorry for *me*?"

"You think you're winning, but in the end you're going to die too. Because no one lives forever. When it's your turn, you'll have reason to be afraid of dying."

During the oxygen crisis, I'd finally been able to believe the most important thing a person can learn. Dying doesn't

AMBUSH
111

mean the end, so dying isn't the worst thing that can happen to a person. Not when God is waiting.

He sneered. "Spare me that faith nonsense. No one has power over me. I'll do what I want for as long as I want. And that will last for years and years after you've turned to dust."

Dr. Jordan turned his back on me. He had no reason to worry that I could do anything. Not from my wheelchair. Not unless he fell into my lap.

I had to twist my head to watch him step over to his computer. The satellite feed ran through a program on the computer. If the computer started properly, I truly was dead. I knew I'd need God's help through the last moments of neuron gun torture.

But if the computer wouldn't operate . . .

He snapped on the power button. I was hoping for a sizzle or pop, hoping the paper clip I'd struggled to lay across the power relay inside the computer box would short-circuit the system.

And I got far more than I hoped for.

Instead of a sizzle or pop, the entire computer screen exploded, sending a surge of blue light toward Dr. Jordan's stomach!

I think it was more the surprise than the electrical surge that threw him back.

He staggered toward me with a small yelp. He bumped into my wheelchair and began to fall.

Right across my lap!

What I wanted to do was push forward and fall out of my wheelchair and roll on top of him and somehow wrestle with him until he gave up.

But his weight changed that. He'd locked the brakes on my wheelchair and, braced from going backward, it flipped forward with his weight. Because I was trying to push forward too, it gave extra force.

Dr. Jordan's head hit the edge of the desk with a sickening thump. He tumbled to the floor, groaned once as he flopped a few times, then collapsed completely. Unconscious.

"His neuron gun," Ashley said after a second of silent disbelief. "Can you get it from him?"

I, too, stared in disbelief. "Won't work for me. Each gun is matched to the fingerprints programmed into it."

"We've got to do something. Fast. He could wake up any second."

I stared at Dr. Jordan for another couple of seconds. His glasses had fallen from his face.

"Can you slide your chair this way?" I asked Ashley. "I think I have an idea."

CHAPTER 22

Ten minutes later, Blaine Steven walked into Dr. Jordan's office.

I couldn't see him. I could only hear his first words to Dr. Jordan. His voice was muffled to me. "I came as soon as possible. What is—?"

I knew why he'd stopped in surprise because I could picture what he saw.

Ashley was standing near the computer with the busted screen. I was slumped in my wheelchair, my head down, in the robot activation zone of concentration, with the transmitter connected to my neck-plug. And Dr. Jordan sat in the chair where Ashley had been taped to the armrests. Only now Dr. Jordan was the one whose wrists were taped in place, his right hand holding the neuron gun, pointed at the doorway.

"Dr. Jordan!" Steven said. "Your face!" There was a pause. "Your nose!"

I could picture, too, exactly how it appeared to Blaine Steven. Dr. Jordan's nose had been duct-taped shut. That way he couldn't sneeze or snort out a blast of air. Otherwise, the ant-bot would be gone, and there would be no way to force Dr. Jordan to do as he'd been told.

I waited for him to follow the first step of our instructions. A loud, angry yell reached me.

Step 1. Hit Steven in the legs with the neuron gun. Right on schedule.

"Shut up," Dr. Jordan told Steven. Dr. Jordan's voice was loud to me. Very loud. "And do exactly as I say. Ashley is going to tape your hands together. Let her do it, or I'll be forced to fire another shot."

"That's a . . . that's a . . ."

"Yes," Dr. Jordan said. "It's a neuron gun."

"But. . . but . . ."

I wasn't surprised Blaine Steven sounded muffled to me or that Dr. Jordan's voice was loud and echoed weirdly. I was, after all, in Dr. Jordan's sinuses. That's right. Up his nose.

Seconds later I heard Ashley. "It's done, Tyce. He's taped. Wrists and ankles."

Good. Dr. Jordan was taped in his chair. Steven was sitting on the floor, also taped and helpless. They couldn't do anything to Ashley now.

"Give me the computer code that disables all the neuron guns," Dr. Jordan said to Steven. "If you do, I'll send Ashley to your office, where she'll enter the code. And then you'll be safe."

"Have you lost your mind?" came Steven's voice. I imagined his face growing red with rage underneath his thick gray hair.

"Give me the code," Dr. Jordan said, "or I'll have to shoot again."

"Jordan," Steven said, "if I disable your gun, all the neuron guns under the dome will be disabled. What's gotten into you?"

Ashley giggled. "That's a better question than you know."

If the ant-bot inside Dr. Jordan's nose had been capable of giggling, I'd have done it too.

Ashley continued to speak. "Tyce, give Dr. Jordan a reminder of why he should obey us."

I did. Reaching out a robot arm, I pounded once inside the darkness.

Dr. Jordan moaned.

While Dr. Jordan had been unconscious, Ashley had moved her chair close enough to me so I could rip the tape off her wrists. I'd helped her as much as I could to move him into the chair, and she had quickly taped Dr. Jordan's wrists together, then taken the ant-bot and placed it on his upper lip.

I'd plugged in with the mini-transmitter and, in control of the ant-bot, had gone straight up Dr. Jordan's nose, past the nose hairs that seemed like fence posts. Then Ashley had taped his nose so he couldn't blow me out.

Let me be the first to say that the inside of someone's nose is as gooey and slimy as you can imagine. But I hadn't been able to think of anything nearly as effective. I'd traveled as far up his nose as possible, then waited for him to wake.

Minutes later, when he finally grunted himself back to consciousness, Ashley had informed him of his situation. From inside the nasal passage, the ant-bot's audio sensors had let me hear her threaten him.

"It's very elementary, Dr. Jordan. If the ant-bot goes up any farther, it can penetrate your brain. You don't want that, do you? Tyce, let him know you've got the ant-bot in there."

That's when I'd done it the first time. Begun hammering the sensitive tissue of his sinus passage with both robot arms. He'd understood the message.

Then Ashley had given him the rest of his instructions, beginning with a call to bring in Blaine Steven.

It had taken only one hit on the inside of his nasal passage to convince Dr. Jordan he needed to follow the rest of the instructions.

I heard another yelp. This one from Blaine Steven again.

As instructed earlier, Dr. Jordan must have shot him in the shoulder. Briefly I felt sorry for Steven. I knew what it felt like to be hit by a neuron gun.

"Now do you understand I'm serious?" I heard Dr. Jordan ask. "Give me the code to disable the guns."

"Yes! Yes!" Steven whined. "I understand. You can have the code."

He gave us the right one, the first time.

Which made the next part a lot easier.

CHAPTER 23

"Hello," I said to Dad. "Can you hear me?"

His head spun up and down and side to side, just like I'd done when I'd first heard the ant-bot's voice. I wished I could see his expression. But I was controlling the ant-bot, perched on his shoulder, lighter than a fly. And with only two lights burning in the entire large meeting room, I was nearly invisible on his jumpsuit. I was far too close to see his face.

"Can you hear me?" I repeated. From Dr. Jordan's office, it had taken half an hour to reach the meeting room with the ant-bot. I'd gotten lost twice. Going down corridors that seem two miles wide is a confusing thing.

"I can hear you," he whispered with hesitation. "Unless I'm losing my mind. But who are *you*?"

In any other situation, I'd have been tempted to have

fun with this. But I resisted. I was certain the hostages would all be safe soon enough, but I knew too well that Rawling was still stuck under tons of rock. The sooner the scientists and techies took control of the dome, the sooner the rescue attempt could begin.

"The guards can't stop you now," I said. "Their guns won't work."

Again, Dad's head spun from side to side. "Is this some ventriloquist joke? Who's playing games?"

"Dad," I said, "it's Tyce. Really. I'd tell you where I am, but I'm afraid you'd knock me off as you look for me."

"Tyce?" he asked. "Tyce?"

Before I could answer, Mom's voice interrupted. "Honey, quit mumbling. You'll wake the others around us."

Dad said nothing. I could guess what was going through his mind. If he told Mom he was answering some voice that came to him from the darkness, she'd think he'd suddenly gone crazy.

"I'm real," I told Dad, and then I used the words he always said to me. "Trust me."

"Did you hear that?" he asked Mom. "It's a voice!"

"You're dreaming. Go back to sleep." She patted his back and nearly knocked me off his shoulder.

Time to get serious, before the ant-bot was hurt.

"I know this is hard to believe, but it *is* Tyce," I said. I needed to come up with something he knew only I could know. "The last time we spoke, I was trying to feed you live video from the cave-in."

There was a pause, and then, "Tyce?"

"You've got to trust me. The neuron guns won't fire anymore. Wake everyone up. It's 200 of you against 6 of them. They don't have a chance. Then come and get me from Dr. Jordan's office."

Dad groaned. "How can I believe a voice in the dark?"

"It's Project 3. A miniaturized robot called an ant-bot. Don't move. I'll pinch your neck to show you this is real."

I did.

He laughed in the darkness. "Tyce!"

"It's 200 against 6," I said one more time. "All you need to do is walk up there and ask one of the guards to shoot you. When everybody sees that his gun doesn't work, the fight will be over."

And that was it.

Except for the cave-in.

CHAPTER 24

During the first crisis that hit the dome, Mom asked me to keep a journal so Earth people would know what it was like to live on Mars. Even though we survived the oxygen crisis, Mom insisted I keep writing about what happens on Mars. She has a good point—no one else in the solar system can say they grew up on this planet. At least not yet. And she says that my journals will at least let me look back when I'm an old man and remember everything a lot easier.

Even though Mom's right, there have been times I complained to her about writing my journal entries. I'd much rather be up at the telescope or working with the robot bodies.

I've decided, though, that I'll never complain again.

Here I am, parked in front of my computer, when only 24 hours earlier I was a prisoner in a storage room, afraid of what might happen to me and my parents and the other scientists under the dome, and especially worried about the cave-in.

It is great to be safe. With my biggest problem being what words to put on a blank computer screen. I could be there again, in front of the piled-up rocks of the cave-in, frantically scared that once we dug through, we would find Rawling and the other three dead.

I closed my eyes and thought about what it was like to be there. When I was ready, I began to type.

09.24.2039

If the rescue team consisted of techies in space suits, the oxygen and water of the men trapped by all that rock would have run out long before those techies could have reached them.

Instead, the men were rescued by robots. It became the Mars Project's best argument for the use of robot bodies controlled by humans like me or Ashley.

We began the rescue attempt early in the morning after the scientists and techies had locked up Steven, Jordan, and the guards. The temperature beneath the jet-black Martian sky had dropped to minus 150 degrees Fahrenheit. Wind had picked up, making it even colder.

But Ashley and I were back in the dome, miles away, warm and comfortable and relaxed. Relaxed, except for our minds. Connected by the remotes to our robot bodies, we were concentrating as hard as if we were in a marathon video game. What was better, we were working at it together.

At our direction, all those miles away from the dome, the robot bodies picked up rocks and threw them backward far faster than any human could work. We were helped by two things. First, the robots could lift rocks six times heavier than any Olympian weight lifter. Second, because of the reduced gravity on Mars, even the heaviest of rocks were within the load capabilities of the robots. And unlike human bodies, the robots didn't get tired. A platform buggy stood nearby, with techies ready to replace the robot batteries.

The robots worked out there, side by side, for 15 hours straight, taking breaks only when Ashley and I got too tired to concentrate.

Then, in the 16th hour, we broke through.

Rawling and the other three were in a deep pocket of space, close to their last breaths of oxygen.

Dad told us that while Ashley and I were han-dling the robots, the dramatic rescue attempt was captured live on video and transmitted to Earth media sources. All across the Earth, people watched as Rawling got to his feet and hugged my robot.

Dad says that one image was enough to earn renewed support for the Mars Project and for the budget it would take to develop the robot bodies even more.

Dr. Jordan and Blaine Steven never did get their chance for worldwide attention, but the robots did.

And I have to admit, I liked that!

CHAPTER 25

"It was a setup from the beginning," Rawling said, scratching his short, dark hair that was streaked with gray. "The bombs were in one of the packs. If we hadn't set them against the side of the cave before going in deeper, we would have died instantly."

Rawling and I sat at the telescope on the upper floor of the dome. It was good to see him healthy after wondering if I'd ever see him alive again.

"Dr. Jordan wanted you out of the dome before he began his takeover."

"Exactly," Rawling said. "I should have been suspicious when he insisted that the search needed a medical person. But his position gave him even more authority than the dome director."

I stared upward through the dome at the incredibly black sky of a Martian night. "You won't have to worry about him anymore, huh?"

"Wrong, Tyce."

He said it so sharply that I snapped my head back.

"Think about it. Jordan nearly engineered civil war back on Earth. It's not something he could do without help. And then there are the others you've told me about. Tomorrow we're going to learn everything we can from Ashley. I think there's a lot more to worry about."

Rawling was right. I had plenty of questions too. Because of the cave-in rescue operation—with both Ashley and me controlling the big robots to help move rock—things had been too frantic for me to ask her about anything. Including how she'd survived the Hammerhead space torpedo crash.

Tomorrow. Not only would we talk to Ashley, but tomorrow marked the last day I'd see my dad for three years. Tomorrow night the shuttle headed back to Earth. With Blaine Steven and Dr. Jordan along as prisoners.

"Tyce?" Rawling broke into my thoughts. "Look."

He pointed. I didn't need the telescope to know what it was.

Earth.

"Must be strange," I said. "Seeing it hang there night after night, with all your memories of growing up there."

Rawling laughed. "No more strange than your seeing it

hang there night after night, being the only human in history never to have spent any time there."

"Yeah," I said softly, "it is strange."

"Probably be even more strange seeing it for the first time."

"Yeah," I said, "it would be."

"Not *would*, Tyce. *Will*."

I wasn't sure I understood. "It *will* be strange to see it for the first time?"

Rawling patted my shoulder. "Tomorrow night. You and Ashley will be on the ship with your dad."

"What!"

"For the Mars Project to survive, we need a lot of questions answered. And Mars isn't the place to find those answers. You will go, won't you? I've already talked with your parents about it, and even your mom agrees that she wants you to go."

I hardly heard him. I was staring at that ball of white and blue, 50 million miles away.

Earth.

JOURNAL
TWO

CHAPTER 1

Asteroid.

I used to have this picture in my mind that an asteroid collision meant a rock the size of a mountain ramming a planet or moon at full speed. That the impact would have the power of 10 nuclear bombs. That there would be a massive crater and earthquakes and maybe even parts of the planet or moon splitting off to spin back into space.

Not with this asteroid.

At the most, it had been half the size of a pea. Barely more than space dust. If it had been headed toward Earth, the friction of its high-speed entrance into the atmosphere would have burned it in a brief flare of glory. Anyone seeing it from the ground—and they would have, because even a pea-size asteroid throws a lot of light when it burns—might have wished upon a star.

It had not hit Earth.

It had hit our spaceship, over three-quarters into its 50-million-mile journey from Mars to Earth. It wasn't like running into an iceberg. We hadn't felt the impact inside the ship. But instantly alarm bells had started to clang, waking all nine of us inside and throwing us into emergency mode.

The tiny piece of intergalactic rock had punctured the outer hull, and now valuable oxygen bled into the vacuum of space. Worse, like a tiny stream of water wearing through soggy paper, the hole was growing far too quickly.

It was too dangerous to suit someone up and send him out attached by a safety cable. Which meant I was the one to step into outer space.

Well, not me. But my robot body, because it didn't need the protective clumsiness of a space suit.

I was actually still inside the ship, my brain hooked up by computer to the robot controls. Everything that the robot body sensed, however, reached me as if it were my own body out there.

The robot body was connected to the ship by a safety cable, and it floated and bobbed as I tried to find the source of the leak at the back part of the hull. The view beyond the ship was incredible. We were headed directly toward the sun, and even at some 120 million miles away, it still seemed like the center of the universe.

It did not look yellow. Human eyes need an atmosphere to filter colors, and out here in space, there was no atmosphere. Instead, it was a circle of incredible brightness.

Earth was close enough now that I could see it clearly too. Not in front of the sun. That would have been like looking into a floodlight and trying to see a marble glued to the bulb. No, Earth was off to the side of the sun, and it reflected light as purely as the moon on a dark night.

As a backdrop in all directions, millions and millions of pinpricks showed the light of stars and galaxies. It boggled my mind to think that some of those tiny dots were actually clusters of thousands of stars.

"Tyce? Find anything?"

This was my dad's voice coming through the radio. Not that I needed reminding of the urgency of my mission. If the hole in the hull exploded, all of us inside were dead.

"Nothing yet," I said. "Hang on."

Sunlight caught the rounded hull at an angle that showed me a small dent in the perfect titanium skin.

"Think I found it," I said. "Just in front of one of the hydrogen tanks."

I heard Dad gasp. "You mean it hits us a couple feet farther back and . . ."

Pressure inside the hydrogen tanks was easily 1,000

times higher than pressure inside the spaceship. If the asteroid pea had hit the tank, we would have blown apart into space dust.

"I will be careful," I said. "Promise."

I'd been handling a robot for years, so I wasn't worried about how to move the robot arms and hands and fingers. What I was worried about was the welding torch in the robot's right hand.

My job was to seal on a thin square of titanium about the size of a human's palm, like slapping a bandage over a cut. Except it wasn't that simple.

In the fingers of my robot's left hand was a thin rod of titanium alloy. Because it wasn't pure titanium, it melted at a slightly lower temperature than titanium. I needed to touch the rod and the flame of the welding torch together at the edge of the titanium patch, then melt the tip of the rod so that liquid titanium alloy dribbled over the edge of the patch. As the titanium alloy cooled and solidified again, it would form a seal. Almost like using a glue gun. Once I'd sealed off all sides of the square patch, my job would be finished. Trouble was, the welding torch flame generated heat at over 2,400 degrees Fahrenheit. And I hadn't used a welding torch much.

In fact, this was only my second time.

My first had been on Mars, under the dome, in practice sessions with Rawling. That was over 40 million miles away.

I didn't give myself any more time to worry. This hole had to be sealed. Immediately.

I let myself drift closer to the hull. The robot wheels made a dull clank as they hit the hull. It wasn't a sound that reached the audio components of the robot's body, however. Sound can't travel through a vacuum. Instead, I heard it through the slight vibrations that traveled up the robot body.

I was ready. The titanium patch had a temporary glue to keep it in place. I pushed the patch down, and the glue held. Under the lights of millions of stars, I began to weld.

What I couldn't adjust to was the intensity of the flame's light. "Dad," I said into the radio, "you need to roll the ship a little so I am not in the shadows."

The sun was on the other side. Its light would make it easier for me to see what I needed to do.

Seconds later, the ship rolled. Just slightly. In space, it takes too much fuel to overcorrect any sudden movements.

It also takes very little change of direction for the movement to be felt. The robot body started to slide along the hull.

Without thinking—as if I were in gravity instead of outer space—I put out a hand to balance myself. The robot's right hand. The one with the torch.

The hand hit the hull, and the torch bumped loose.

This wasn't a total disaster. In the floating weightlessness of space, I could catch it before it went another 10 feet.

Except two feet away was the hydrogen tank.

I made a slow-motion grab for the torch, but it flipped end over end, in agonizing slowness, just out of reach.

I could see it happening but was helpless to stop it.

The torch flame touched the side of the hydrogen tank. All 2,400 degrees Fahrenheit of flame concentrated on high-pressure gas inside. The metal of the tank glowed briefly.

Silently I screamed. But it was too late.

Before I could think any more thoughts, all existence disappeared in a blinding flash far brighter than any star.

CHAPTER 2

I spoke into darkness. "Dad, I've got a headache."

I could easily picture where I was. In the robot lab on the *Moon Racer* spaceship. The spaceship got its name because when it was first built, people said it would easily outrace the moon, which it could. The lab held a computer and a bed. I was on that bed, where my spine plug was able to make an X-ray wave connection to the computer hard drive.

The real robots—there were two—were stored in a cargo bay that gave them immediate access to the exterior of the ship. Although I had used my robot frequently on the surface of Mars, the only reason the robots would be needed during the *Moon Racer*'s journey to Earth was during an emergency situation.

"Headache?" Dad chuckled. "You're lucky you don't have

more than that. Welding torches and high-pressure hydrogen fuel tanks don't make for a good mix. I was monitoring your progress in here. You of all people know that the virtual-reality software doesn't mess around."

I knew that Dad was holding the headset, which he had already removed. It had been blocking all sound from reaching my ears. Arms at my side, I was still strapped to the laboratory bed and needed him to remove the blindfold and straps.

"On the trip to Earth—I mean the real trip to Earth—the chances of hitting an asteroid are one in billions, right?" I said defensively. "And then the chances of a puncture near the fuel tank are . . . are . . ."

Dad removed my blindfold, and I blinked a couple of times. His smiling face loomed down at me. He had dark blond hair, like mine, and a large frame. I only hope that someday I'll grow up to be as big as he is.

"Tyce," he answered, his face now serious, "that's the whole point of these virtual-reality training programs. To prepare you for any situation, no matter how unlikely. If for some reason you are called for any duty, you can't afford mistakes."

He unstrapped me from the bed. I sat up.

"I'm sorry," I said. I meant it. Dad was 100 percent correct. After all, he had to be. He was the *Moon Racer*'s pilot, the one we all trusted with our lives. "Could you let me try another run this afternoon?"

His smile returned. "That would take you away from your mathematics, wouldn't it?"

"Much more important to know how to save a spaceship than it is to deal with logarithmic derivatives and triple integrals."

"Perhaps." Dad's grin grew wider. "But I was thinking of Ashley. I was getting the impression that she enjoyed the chance to do schoolwork with you."

I coughed. "She just needs a little help, that's all."

Dad laughed.

I pushed off the bed and began to float in the weightlessness. This was one thing I loved about space travel. I didn't need my wheelchair.

"Don't let her fool you. I've seen the background report on her. The worst grade she ever got in math was a 95 percent." Dad rubbed my hair. "And your best grade has been . . . ?"

"So I don't like math that much," I said.

I reached for my comp-board. It was floating beside the bed, where I had left it before the virtual-reality robot session. Dad had asked me to bring it but hadn't told me why yet.

Comp-board was the term used for keyboard-computer, a portable computer with the screen attached directly to the back of the keyboard. The hard drive was embedded in the left-hand side of the keyboard, with discports on the right-hand side. When I was finished with the computer, all I had to do was fold the keyboard in half, then fold that against the back of the screen, and it would become a small rectangle about the size of a book. Smaller ones were available, but most people preferred a decent-size screen. Under the dome, the comp-board actually docked into my desktop computer, letting me access the comp-board hard drive but giving me access to a bigger screen.

"She's really that good in math?" I asked.

"Uh-huh," Dad said. "So maybe you should figure out why she always asks you to help her."

To give me free use of my hands, I attached the folded-up comp-board to a latch on my belt. I grabbed a handhold—they were placed all through the ship to give passengers a way to travel in the weightlessness—and followed Dad out of the robot lab. We traveled down the inner corridor of the *Moon Racer*.

"Where are we headed?" I asked.

"I need to tweak some of the autopilot controls," Dad answered. "Our mainframe computer has been a little cranky lately. But we need to make a quick stop first."

"Where?"

"I know you're trying to change the subject." He laughed. "Let's get back to math."

"Math?" I tried to sound innocent.

"Ashley wants *you* to learn the math better," Dad answered. "Whatever lies ahead of you, I'm guessing it will involve exploration of the solar system. You're going to need advanced calculus to get any kind of education that allows for space travel."

"If she wants me to learn better, why doesn't *she* teach *me*?"

He laughed again. "She is. Sometimes the best way to learn is by figuring something out for yourself, then teaching it to someone else. By asking questions that she already knows the answers to, she's making you do exactly that."

"Oh."

"She might have another reason too."

"What's that?" I asked.

"All I'm saying is that she sure seems to smile a lot when she's around you."

"Huh?"

"You figure it out." Dad stopped in front of a closed hatch that led to a private bunk. The hatch was a circular opening, twice as wide as his shoulders. The "door" to the hatch slid open or shut by entering a code into one of the small keypads—one on the outside and one on the inside. He punched in the five-digit code.

"Hey," I said, "this is Blaine Steven's bunk."

"I know," Dad said. "He wants to talk to you."

"Me? He's already tried to kill me three different times."

CHAPTER 3

The hatch door slid open, and my heart started to pound.

Blaine Steven couldn't be trusted. So why would my dad want me to talk with him?

"I think you should speak to him," Dad said quietly. "He's been asking for you specifically. And this is after months of refusing to speak to anyone on the *Moon Racer*. He also asked that you take your comp-board."

I shook my head. This all seemed so unreal. "You'll wait for me?"

"I'll be right here," he said.

"I'm not sure I want to be alone with him," I said nervously.

"He insisted," Dad said. "And he won't be able to do anything to you as long as you stay out of his reach. Remember that. All you need to do is yell, and I'll be there."

"Thanks," I said. But I still didn't like the idea.

I floated into Blaine Steven's prison bunk. Dad shut the hatch behind me. The clank echoed. It felt like I had been shut into prison myself.

With only a couple of weeks of the journey left, why did Blaine Steven want to see me? And why did he want me to bring my comp-board?

"Hello, Tyce."

The man on the far side of the bunk wore the regulation blue jumpsuit, with one difference. A wide metal band circled his waist. This band was attached to the wall by a short length of cable. It gave him just enough room to reach his e-book and other possessions and take care of his personal needs. Anywhere else but in weightlessness, a leash like this would have been cruel punishment.

"Hello," I answered. Without friendliness. This man had tried to do a lot of damage to the Mars Project. And to me.

"Thanks for coming," the silver-haired man with cold blue eyes said. He looked like a dignified judge. But I knew he used this respectable appearance to fool people.

I shrugged.

"I can understand that you don't feel much like talking with me," he said.

I remembered what it had been like the other times we spoke. When he was director. In his office. Under the dome.

On Mars. Where he had treated me like a blob of mud to be scraped off his shoe. I shrugged again.

"And that's all right. I can do most of the talking if you like." Steven put his finger to his mouth as if he were silencing me. It didn't make sense. I was already silent. He pointed at my computer and gestured for me to give it to him.

I shook my head. How could I trust him with it?

"It is very important that we talk," he said pleasantly. As he spoke, he acted as if he were typing on a keyboard. "I hope you understand that," he said in the same pleasant tone. He put his hands together as if he were begging. Then he pretended to keyboard again.

"I also hope you will feel free to say anything you want to me." Except his actions showed the opposite. Steven violently shook his head, mouthing the word *no*. He pointed to the walls around him and pointed to his ears.

Despite my intense dislike for him, I was curious. Did he mean that I shouldn't speak freely because the walls were listening?

He made the same begging motion as before and pointed at my computer again.

As crazy as this was, I made a decision to find out what he wanted. To play his game, if only for a minute. After all, I knew I could always yell for help and Dad would be there in a flash. "I'm not sure I want to talk to you," I said. But I unfolded the keyboard, popped the screen up, and powered the comp-board. The screen brightened. I opened a new file in a word processing program. "What is there to talk about?"

Making sure I didn't get near Steven, I pushed the comp-board ahead. It floated toward him. He smiled with gratitude.

"I want to ask you about your faith." Steven brought his knees up to give him a support for the comp-board. "Spending all this time alone in prison has given me a lot of time to think."

"Faith?" I asked, shocked.

"I've been thinking about my life. What I've done with it. And what might happen if I die."

This was the last thing I'd expected to talk about with Blaine Steven, the man who didn't seem to have a conscience. Who'd been willing to kill a couple hundred people under the dome to save some key scientists and their illegal experiment.

"I can see the surprise on your face. Take some time to think about your answer." He put his head down and began to type frantically, humming loudly to cover the sound of his fingers on the keyboard.

When he finished, he pushed the comp-board in my direction. It slowly drifted through the bunk, and I reached for it before it floated past me.

Steven put his finger in front of his mouth again. But it was a warning I didn't need. Not after reading the first words he had typed onto the screen.

Don't say anything. I am sure there are listening devices in this bunk.

I lifted my head and nodded at Steven. I read more.

I have vital information about the rebels who are trying to destroy the dome and take over the World United Federation. But I will not give out this information unless I know I will be protected. Which includes your silence. Do you agree?

I typed:

I will remain silent in here.

I wasn't going to make much more of a promise until I knew more. Especially with a man I'd never liked, a man who couldn't be trusted. I pushed the comp-board toward him.

"Faith is important to you, isn't it?" he said in the same pleasant tone. I knew he was speaking for the benefit of the listening device. If there really was one.

"I can't tell you I have all the answers," I said. "But, yes, it is important."

As I spoke, he quickly read my answer and typed one of his own, humming the entire time. He pushed the comp-board back to me.

"I am beginning to see that faith is the most important thing a person can have," Blaine Steven said. "And I would like it if you visited me more often so that we could talk about it."

I hardly heard him as I scanned the screen.

> You know that Dr. Jordan and I are part of the Terratakers rebel group and worked together in the dome to overthrow the World United's control of Mars. But there is someone else of greater power we report to. And far more hidden. Even from me. I now believe this mastermind is on this ship. I can hear strange things happening through the wall. I think Dr. Jordan is working with the mastermind. They want to make sure that I do not survive the trip to Earth.

Through the wall. Dr. Jordan's prison bunk was on the other side of this one.

I typed a question in response.

> *Who is the other person that you say is the mastermind behind the rebels?*

Although I moved closer to Blaine Steven to give him the comp-board, I still made sure I was out of his reach. I waited as he typed frantically.

He gave me the comp-board.

> If I knew who it was, I would tell you. My best guess
> about their plan is an explosive device. But don't limit
> the search for that. If you see anything unusual, be
> suspicious. Find a way to stop them. I will keep my
> other secrets until I'm sure I can trade them for my
> freedom. Or my life.

I typed two words.

> *Explosive device?*

This was Blaine Steven's answer on the screen:

> *I distinctly heard the word* bomb. *Which terrifies
> me. And should terrify you. Because I am not the
> only one they want dead.*

CHAPTER 4

"What are you doing?"

Stuck against the far wall of one of the spaceship's bunk areas, I had little room to move. The bunk was hardly more than a bed on a large shelf, with other smaller shelves below. Each of those shelves had loose netting in front so the objects on them would not float out.

"What are you doing?" came the angry demand again. The man who floated headfirst in the hatchway to the bunk wore the regulation blue jumpsuit. But all I could see were his head and shoulders since the rest of his body hung out in the corridor. I knew he didn't look regulation in any other way. His upper body was an upside-down triangle, his waist narrow and his shoulders and chest so heavily muscled that he barely fit into the hatchway. His neck seemed as wide as his head. Because he cut his dark hair so short, the first thing you noticed about his square face was his ears, which stuck straight out from his head. Not that anyone would ever mention it to him.

Turning my head to look at him was an awkward move, considering I was on my back. Or on my side. Or upside down. It's hard to tell in the weightlessness of interplanetary travel since all positions feel the same. But in relationship to the ceiling, I clung to a handhold bar on the wall, with a vacuum tube floating beside me. So I probably looked like a fly, with my legs tucked beneath me in the cramped quarters of the bunk.

What made me look like a thief, however, was the fact that I had undone the netting of his shelves.

"What are you doing?" Lance Evenson repeated one more time. As his body showed, he was a workout freak and had a reputation for using his size to frighten people. It worked. I *was* frightened at his anger. "And tell me why you're in my bunk area without my permission!"

I wasn't going to tell him I was looking for a bomb. No, when Dad had sent me out with a vacuum tube, he'd been very clear we needed to keep it a secret. One, as Dad had warned, we did not want to let the traitor know we knew about the bomb. And two, we didn't want to panic the others.

"I'm . . . I'm . . . cleaning." I pointed at the vacuum tube. It was about as long and as wide as my arm, with a powerful little motor hidden inside. It was designed to pick up crumbs and dust that hung in the air.

"I can see you're cleaning," he snapped. "What I want to know is why you have invaded my privacy and what you expect to clean among my personal possessions on the shelf."

Although his official title was chief computer technician, Lance Evenson's job was considered to be far, far more crucial than the duties of most techies. Computers were the lifeblood of space exploration. In the dome on Mars and on a spaceship. Power equipment, machines, engines—all depended on computers. Positional information and the calculation of space orbits depended on computers. All communications depended on computers. And all those computers depended on the chief computer technician for maintenance and repairs. No one reached the status of chief computer technician without years of training and experience. It was easier to become a doctor than a chief computer technician. And for good reason. Doctors were responsible for one life at a time. A chief computer technician was responsible for every life under the dome. Or on a spaceship.

"My dad asked me to vacuum everywhere," I said. "He told me it's part of regular duties on a long flight like ours. Good as the filters are, he wants to stay on top of the dust and particles so there's absolutely no chance of clogging anything important."

"Humph," Lance said. "That's news to me. I don't remember doing it on my trip to Mars."

Which had been nearly 15 Earth years ago. Lance had been on the Mars Dome since it had been established. This was his first trip back to Earth. Having a man of his knowledge and expertise to help if anything went wrong was fortunate for the rest of us.

"News to me too," I answered. "I'd rather be in a simulation software game right now. But this is my first flight, and how can I disagree with my dad? Especially because he's the pilot."

I said that as a way to remind Lance that he, too, had to follow the pilot's orders. Chief computer technician or not, in space the first rule was that the pilot had total authority.

"Fine, then." Lance pulled himself through the hatchway and, with a slight push, sent himself toward me. He put out an arm and stopped himself against the wall beside me. "Give me the vacuum tube. I'll take care of it."

"I don't mind doing it," I said, trying to shrink back from the closeness of his large body. "I'm nearly done in here anyway."

"I don't care. I want you out of my bunk."

"Yes, sir," I said. I pushed off the wall, toward the hatch. I grabbed the handhold bars on each side. As I began to pull my body forward, like a worm about to squeeze out of a hole, Lance's voice stopped me.

"Pilot's order or not," Lance said harshly, "I don't want to catch you in here again. If there's something you need in my bunk, you talk to *me* first. And I'll be telling the same thing to your father. Got that?"

"Got it," I said.

"Good. Then get out of my sight. And close the hatch door behind you."

I poked my head through the hatchway and looked both directions up and down the corridor. Although there were only nine people on the ship, we'd all learned early to check before shooting out of our bunks. Weightless or not, collisions still hurt.

Once the rest of my body was out of the hatch, I flipped over, like a fish doing a somersault in water. I secured the hatch, grabbed the nearest handhold bar, and shoved off to find Dad. He'd want to know about this.

Lance Evenson was the only person so far to react like this. So I was willing to bet that he was hiding something.

CHAPTER 5

Of the entire ship, my favorite area was the navigation cone, which formed the ship's nose. For two reasons. One, the telescope was located there, and I'd spent every evening that I could at the telescope under the dome on Mars. And two, because standing in the cone was like being perched in outer space.

The cone was the only place with a view. The rest of the ship behind it was made of a titanium alloy, and the bunks and work areas had no windows. They were lit by the pale whiteness of low-energy argon tubes set into the walls.

The cone sat in front, where it looked like an awkward addition. But because there's no air in space or any gravity to pull a structure apart, the ship was designed much differently than if it had to fly in an atmosphere.

Essentially the entire ship was a large circular tube, moving sideways through the vacuum of space. The outer part of this large tube held the docking port, two emergency escape pods, an exercise room, all the passenger bunks, and work-area compartments. The inner part of the circle formed a corridor, which we traveled by grabbing handholds and pushing forward or backward, entering the bunks or work areas through circular hatches with slide-away covers. From this corridor, four main hatches led to tubes that extended downward like spokes and met at a center hub. From this center hub one short tube led backward to the pyramid-shaped, ion-drive engine. Another short tube led forward to the pyramid-shaped navigation cone.

Here in the navigation cone, the titanium structure of the rest of the ship had been replaced by material that looked and functioned like glass but was thousands of times stronger and more expensive. All the walls of the pyramid were made of this space glass, including the floor. The computer and control console sat on this glass floor, as did the pilot's seat. That's why I liked it so much. Pushing from the hub into the navigation cone made it seem like a person was floating directly into clear outer space. This sensation frightened some people, but because in gravity situations I spent so much time in a wheelchair, I loved the illusion of freedom.

This time, however, pushing from the confined tube of

the hub into the navigation cone to visit my dad gave me little pleasure.

Not with the news I had to deliver.

"Nothing," I told him. "I found nothing unusual except one cranky chief computer technician."

I explained to Dad what had happened during my search.

Sitting before a computer screen and the ship's controls, Dad leaned back, hands locked behind his head. His face showed little expression as he listened.

"What do you think?" I asked when I finished. "Sounds suspicious, doesn't it?"

"First, we don't know for sure that there is a bomb or a plot. Remember who the information is coming from. Second, even if there is a plot, I highly doubt Lance Evenson could be part of a master plot like this. And even if he did intend to hide a bomb, we'd never find it. He's brilliant."

"But he made it clear he didn't want me in his bunk. That must mean something."

Dad grinned. "It means he's one of the most stubborn, opinionated, and cranky men I know. If you'd been in there trying to give him money, he still would have kicked you out. Just because you didn't ask permission to go into his bunk ahead of time."

I wanted to protest. But before I could say anything,

Ashley arrived, bobbing through the air, holding a vacuum tube identical to mine.

I was still getting used to it, watching the way that everyone moved in weightless conditions. Whichever direction a person pushed, he or she would continue to move in that direction until hitting something, grabbing something to stop, or pushing off in a different direction.

Most bizarre of all was what happened to liquids that spilled. In gravity situations, of course, all of it fell straight down and splattered. Not on a spaceship. Droplets would move slowly in every direction, in big and little blobs, and with enough time and patience you could herd the droplets by capturing them in a container. (This made bathroom arrangements very interesting.)

"Mr. Sanders," Ashley said after her quick hello to both of us, "are you sure this isn't some kind of trick that you and Rawling decided to play on me and Tyce?"

Dad raised an eyebrow. I admired the move and had been practicing it myself. But only when no one was around.

"What I mean," she said, "is that maybe this is a way to fool us into cleaning the ship. You know, getting us into every corner and hidden space with a vacuum tube."

Dad shook his head with a sad smile. "I wish it was."

Ashley sighed. She floated on her side in midair, as if she were on an invisible sofa. "I was afraid of that."

"Nothing, huh?" I asked. I was on my stomach in midair,

facing her and Dad. The constant hum of the air circulators surrounded us, as the filters removed carbon dioxide and replaced it with oxygen generated from special tanks.

"Nothing. I'm scared of finding it. And scared of *not* finding it," she said, pushing back the short black hair that floated around her face.

I knew exactly what she meant. We absolutely had to find the bomb to have a chance of surviving this trip. But if we did find it, would we discover that it couldn't be moved or safely disarmed?

"I'll agree with you," Dad answered intensely. Then he frowned. "What's worse, I'm not sure we have much time."

Dad unlocked his hands and leaned forward. Normally any movement like that in weightlessness meant he would keep falling forward unless he grabbed at the armrests of his chair. But because pilots needed to be stable during any maneuvers, small Velcro patches on the seat of his jumpsuit kept him attached to his chair.

"It's like this," he said. "It's unlikely that whoever planted the bomb is suicidal. Agreed?"

"Agreed," Ashley and I said together.

"Which means he is not going to explode the bomb unless he can get away."

"Agreed," we said again.

"So think about our escape pods."

I was beginning to understand. There were nine of us on

the *Moon Racer*. Each of the escape pods was capable of holding 10 people, supplying them with enough food and water and oxygen for 3 weeks. The *Moon Racer* carried 2 escape pods because it often had up to 20 passengers.

"If he's going to blow up the *Moon Racer*," I said, "he'll use the space pod to escape first. That means he needs to be less than three weeks away from any shuttle that can pick him up."

"Exactly," Dad said. "If I were him, I'd use the *Moon Racer*'s direction and momentum. Once we were three weeks from arrival, I'd eject in the direction of Earth and turn on my distress signal in the escape pod. Any one of dozens of Earth-Moon shuttles would be able to pick up the pod once it's within orbit range."

Ashley's lips tightened and her almond-shaped eyes flashed. "And we are now within the escape pods' range of Earth."

"Give or take a couple of days," Dad said. "The important thing is to keep this among the three of us and to find different ways to search."

I knew what I'd be doing. Watching Lance Evenson. And I had an idea how to do it.

I caught Dad frowning at me, as if he were reading my mind.

I was wrong.

"Just had an idea," he said. "Did either of you check our escape pods for a bomb?"

My eyes widened. "Hadn't thought of it."

"I'll check them both," Dad said quickly, as he turned on the autopilot controls and then got out of his seat. "If the bomb is in one, he must intend to use the other."

"Finding it in an escape pod would solve the problem, wouldn't it?" I said. "If we can't disarm the bomb, we'll just eject the pod into space and not care where it blows up."

Great solution. Except, as it turned out, I was wrong about that too.

CHAPTER 6

"You know what's weird?" Ashley asked me.

Except for the usual background humming of the *Moon Racer*'s air circulation units, it was quiet. She and I were at our usual early evening meeting place. In the *Moon Racer*'s observation quarters.

It was the same size as the robot lab, but there was no computer or X-ray receiver. Instead, a telescope tube fit through the upper panels and extended beyond the ship. Eight months to Mars and eight months back is a lot of travel time, and Earth scientists use a lot of the recorded information from this telescope. After all, there's no atmosphere to interfere with the view, and the camera shots and real-time visuals from this telescope are amazing.

I spent hours here, looking at clusters of galaxies and

supernovas and the different planets of the solar system. It never failed to stagger me, wondering where all this beauty came from. It never failed to lead me to thoughts about God.

"I'll bite," I said. I was floating upside down beneath the telescope tube, staring at Mars, wondering what Mom was doing there right now. And if Rawling had started a new project without me. The swirls of red made me homesick. "What's weird?"

"Just yesterday, Dr. Jordan wanted to ask me questions."

"What!" I would have jumped if there were any gravity. I switched my attention from Mars to Ashley.

"Don't look at me like that. It's not that big a deal. I was going down the corridor, and Luke Daab was doing some maintenance work on the hatch door to Dr. Jordan's prison bunk. Luke said Dr. Jordan wanted to ask me a question. I didn't even go inside. I just stuck my head through the hatch. Dr. Jordan was cabled to the wall, of course. And Luke Daab was right beside me, so I knew I was safe."

"What did he ask?" I didn't feel any better because of what I'd heard. Blaine Steven was bad enough, but compared to the evil Dr. Jordan, Blaine seemed like an innocent baby.

"About my escape. You know, the Hammerhead."

"Did you tell him?"

"Not a chance. You know it makes me sick to even think of him. I hope he wonders for the rest of his life. Especially since you know how easy it was."

I did. The test had taken place from a shuttle that orbited Mars. Just before the test began, Ashley had loaded a spare space suit into the Hammerhead. Because only the dark helmet and visor were visible to us inside the shuttle, it looked like she was at the controls. Instead, she had remained inside the cargo bay, speaking to us as if she were actually on the space torpedo. She controlled the first part of the Hammerhead's flight, long enough to set its course for impact on the distant moon. It fooled all of us, including Dr. Jordan, into thinking she had died during the crash. After the shuttle landed on Mars, she sneaked out of the cargo bay unnoticed and hid in the dome until it was finally safe to appear again.

"Oh. Was that all he wanted?"

"That was his only question."

"You're right," I said. "That *is* weird."

I should have given it more thought. Dr. Jordan didn't do anything without a reason. But I noticed the look on Ashley's face. She was scared.

"It'll be all right," I said.

"How do you know what I'm thinking?"

"You're thinking about the others in the experimental group." The kids that Ashley and I were supposed to try to find. That was why we were headed back to Earth.

She gave me a small smile. "You know me pretty well."

Ashley was part of a small group of Earth kids who had been operated on to be able to handle robot controls remotely.

Dr. Jordan had forced her to go to Mars with a simple and effective threat. If Ashley didn't do exactly as she was told—including maintaining the pretense that she was his daughter—the kids in the experimental group would be killed. That's why she'd made it look like the Hammerhead failure killed her.

"It'll be okay," I said. "Dr. Jordan and Blaine Steven are military prisoners. Word was sent from Mars to keep that highly confidential. Those kids will be all right. I mean, that's why you and I are going back to Earth. To break them loose. They'll be exactly where you left them."

Which was some sort of hidden retreat in the Arizona desert. Once the *Moon Racer* reached the Earth orbit, we would be shuttled to the surface of the planet. After a week to get used to the gravity, Dad would lead us to the retreat, and Ashley would show him and other soldiers the entrance. The plan had full military approval.

"Tyce, those were my friends. All of us have been together, training in virtual reality, as long as we can remember. If my actions hurt them, I'd never forgive myself."

As she spoke, she touched the silver cross on a chain around her neck. It was an earring, and it matched the cross around my neck, which she'd given me once as a friendship gift.

A thought hit me. "You know what else is weird?"

"What?"

"I've never asked you where you got the silver crosses

from. I'd be surprised if one of the rebel leaders who guarded your experimental group gave them to you. . . ."

Another smile from her, this one sad. "They're from my parents. At least, that's what I was told. I was just a baby when they died in a car crash. That's all that I ever had of them. Not even a photo."

Her sad smile didn't change. "That's why I ended up in the experimental group. Because I was an orphan. Like the others. There was nobody around to wonder where we went or to care what happened to us."

She was thinking about them again. I could tell by her face.

"Really, Ashley," I said softly, "it will be all right."

I didn't add my next thought. *If we make it to Earth.*

CHAPTER 7

It was late at night. At least, it was late in the 24-hour schedule that we followed. Day and night didn't really exist on the spaceship. We were always headed toward the sun, so we really didn't have a day or night.

I floated beside my bed, sitting in a cross-legged position with my comp-board on my lap. I stared at the unfolded screen. Over the last few months of travel—because not much new happened from day to day—I had not spent much time on the comp-board adding to my Mars journal entries.

Part of it was because I didn't want to remind myself of the homesickness I felt whenever I couldn't fall asleep quickly.

Like now, reading one of my first entries on the space trip.

A little over two weeks ago, I was on Mars. Under the dome. Living life in a wheelchair. I'd been born there, and the most I had ever traveled in any direction was 200 miles. Then, with the suddenness of a lightning bolt, I discovered I would be returning to Earth with Dad as he piloted this spaceship on the three-year round-trip to Earth and back to Mars. Although the actual legs of the journey only take eight months to get there and eight months to get back, the planets' orbits have to be aligned correctly in order to make the trip. And that takes three years.

I'd been dreaming of Earth for years.

After all, I was the only human in the history of mankind who had never been on the planet. I'd only been able to watch it through the telescope and wonder about snowcapped mountains and blue sky and rain and oceans and rivers and trees and flowers and birds and animals.

Earth.

When Rawling had told me I was going to visit Earth, I'd been too excited to sleep. Finally I'd be able to see everything I'd only read about under the cramped protection of the Mars Dome, where it never rained, the sky outside was the color of butterscotch, and the mountains were dusty red.

But when it came time to roll onto the shuttle

that would take us to the *Moon Racer*, waiting in orbit around Mars, I had discovered an entirely new sensation. Homesickness. Mars—the dome—was all I knew.

Dozens of technicians and scientists had been there when we left, surprising me by their cheers and affection. Rawling had been there, the second-to-last person to say good-bye, shaking my hand gravely, then giving me a hug.

And the last person?

That had been Mom, biting her lower lip and blinking back tears. It hurt so much seeing her sad—and feeling my own sadness. I'd nearly rolled my wheelchair away from the shuttle. At that moment three years seemed like an eternity. I knew that if an accident happened anywhere along the 100 million miles of travel to Earth and back, I might never see her again.

Mom must have been able to read my thoughts because she'd leaned forward to kiss me and told me to not even dare think about staying. She'd whispered that although she'd miss me, she knew that I was in God's hands, so I wouldn't be alone. She said she was proud of me for taking this big step, and she'd pray every day for the safe return of me and Dad.

The first few nights on the spaceship had not been easy. Alone in my bunk I had stared upward in the darkness for hours and hours, surprised at how much the sensation of homesickness could fill my stomach.

Who would think that a person could miss a place that would kill you if you walked outside without a space suit. . . .

My comp-board bogged down. The arrow kept scrolling down the page, but the letters on the screen lagged behind.

I stopped. This was puzzling. Except for the short time this afternoon with Blaine Steven, this had also happened the last time I used my comp-board. I'd even asked Lance Evenson to check it then, but he'd said it was my imagination.

Except this was definitely not my imagination.

I scrolled farther and finally got to the end of what I had written. As I began to keyboard a new entry, describing the events of this day, the comp-board just as mysteriously began to work at its normal speed.

That was about the only good thing about this bomb threat. It took my mind off how badly I still missed Mom and everyone else on Mars.

I stopped keyboarding and let my thoughts drift off. I was tempted to fold the comp-board right now and try to sleep again, but I knew that once I closed my eyes, my mind would go right back to wondering about the bomb. Would I have any time to realize what was happening when it exploded? How might it feel to get sucked into the vacuum of outer space? And—

Stop! I told myself.

I focused on the keyboard and began to type again.

So who might be the "mastermind" that Blaine Steven told me about? That is, if he wasn't lying to me for some reason. And considering his past record, that's a good possibility. Is the mastermind really on the *Moon Racer*? There aren't that many people on board.

There's me, of course, and Dad and Ashley. Lance Evenson, the chief computer technician. Luke Daab, a maintenance engineer who helped maintain the dome's mechanical equipment during his 15 years on Mars. Susan Fielding, a genetic scientist who spent only three years on Mars. And Jack Tripp, a mining engineer who was returning with a couple tons of rock samples.

There are also two prisoners. Blaine Steven, the ex-director of the dome, and Dr. Jordan, who arrived with Ashley on Mars only three months before leaving again on this ship.

Nine altogether. And if one of them . . .

I stopped typing again.

I couldn't help but wonder if Blaine Steven had been telling the truth. Maybe he just wanted to make trouble. I wouldn't put it past him.

But if someone had actually planted a bomb, my first guess was Lance Evenson. But it would be dumb to make that assumption without at least considering if it could be anyone else.

If Blaine Steven and Dr. Jordan hadn't been securely sealed in their bunks, both of them would have been prime suspects. They'd been working together on Mars for a rebel group on Earth and had nearly succeeded in destroying the whole Mars Project. But neither had been able to leave their bunks, and it would be impossible for either to reach an escape pod. So it couldn't be Steven or Jordan.

Luke Daab? He was a skinny, redheaded guy with a beach ball belly and a nervous laugh. He chewed his fingernails badly too. I couldn't imagine him trying to pull off something like this.

Susan Fielding—chubby with blonde hair—never spoke above a whisper. Although she was older than Dad, she was smaller than Ashley and never went anywhere on the ship without an e-book in her hands or tucked under an arm. I couldn't picture her as the traitor either.

Maybe Jack Tripp, though. He and Dad were about the same age and the same size. Jack had a big red nose, twitchy red eyebrows to match his wiry red hair, and a loud laugh, usually at his own jokes, which weren't that funny.

The trouble with trying to guess, I realized, was that any guess I made was based on appearance only. I didn't really know much else about them.

I looked at my computer screen, barely focusing on the words I'd already written. Then I thought of something as I stared at my journal entry.

Yes! That was it! Ashley and I could interview everybody on this ship. We could write about this trip as a school project or even for an e-magazine. Some Web site somewhere would love to have an article about two kids traveling from Mars to Earth. That would be the excuse Ashley and I would use to ask everyone on board more about themselves.

But we'd have to find the traitor sometime in the next few days.

Great as the idea was, I knew I should clear it with Dad first. This, I figured, was as good a time as any to go over and talk to him about it.

I folded up the computer and placed it behind the netting of the shelf beneath my bed. Scooting out the hatch, I maneuvered my way down the corridor to Dad's hatch.

I knocked first, keeping a tight grip on a nearby handhold so when my knuckles hit his hatch, the counterforce wouldn't float me backward.

"Yes?" Dad answered immediately from the other side.

"It's me."

I heard the *blip-blip-blip-blip-blip* as he entered his code into the keypad. The hatch door slid open with a hiss.

"Come on in," he said.

I did. He closed the hatch behind me.

I didn't like the expression on his face. "Did I wake you?" Usually he was up late, going over ship reports.

"No."

"Good. For a second I thought you were upset."

"I am. But not at you."

Now I really didn't like the expression on his face.

"Tyce," he said gravely, "remember I said I was going to check the escape pods?"

I nodded. "You found the bomb?"

"No, not yet. Worse. Both escape pods have been disabled by a computer malfunction that Lance can't seem to fix. There is no way to leave this ship safely."

CHAPTER 8

"How about one of us uses the ant-bot to find out if Lance Evenson has something hidden in his room?" I asked Ashley.

We were in the exercise room, halfway through the next morning. Ashley sat at a leg-press machine, which, of course, I never used. I sat at a bench-press machine. Sweat covered me. I'd been pushing the weights hard, knowing that once I stepped onto Earth, my muscles would be working against gravity more than double what I'd faced on Mars.

"I thought of that last night as I was falling asleep," she said. "But I don't know if we can."

"Why not?"

"I'm not sure it's physically possible on this spaceship."

"We're both wired," I said. Which we were.

"Still won't work," she said.

I raised an eyebrow. The way that Dad did. At least I thought it was the way Dad did.

Ashley giggled. "You need more practice."

"Huh?"

"With that eyebrow. I saw you the other day. Trying it in a mirror."

"Ant-bot," I said, hoping my face wasn't too red. "Why won't it work?"

"There's no gravity that would allow the ant-bot to crawl." Ashley pointed at a nearby handhold. "You and I are big enough to grab those and pull forward. But the ant-bot would just float around aimlessly. Even if we found a way to let it travel, how are you going to get into Lance's bunk? You don't have the access code to his hatch door. It's not like last time, where your dad was using the mainframe computer to get us into different places on the ship."

"One step ahead of you," I said. "There's another way to get in. Through the air vent. Even without gravity on this ship, there's still air movement. That's why we have the vents. I'm saying we put the ant-bot in the right air vent and let the air blow it all the way down to his bunk. Then we leave it there to watch him later."

"Might work," she said. "Just might work."

"Of course it will. We could try it this afternoon and—" I stopped as someone else floated into the exercise room.

Susan Fielding. In the regulation blue jumpsuit. She had a towel wrapped around her neck. As usual, she had an e-book with her.

"Hello," she said in her quiet voice. "Do you want me to come back later?"

"No," I said quickly. Dad had given Ashley and me permission to work on a feature article. This would be a great time to start learning more about the crew. "In fact, we were hoping to get the chance to spend some time with you. Ashley and I would like to interview you."

"Me?"

I nodded.

"I'm . . . I'm . . . not sure. Is this very important?"

I nodded again. More important than she could guess. Unless, of course, she was the traitor. Then there was nothing for her to guess.

"I was born in Chicago," Susan said.

The three of us floated comfortably beside the weight equipment.

"Both my parents were scientists," she continued. "So it was only natural that I discovered the same kind of interest. I spent 10 years at a university, then another 3 in specialized training for the Mars Project."

I groaned. "Thirteen more years of school."

Ashley elbowed me. I bounced off her elbow and floated

away. I had to find a handhold and use it to push myself back toward them.

"It's not that bad," Susan said, giving me a shy smile. "Not if you love the research and learning like I do."

"No kidding. I mean, genetics. Mom explained the basics to me. To think that scientists are able to engineer—" I snapped my mouth shut so quickly that my teeth clacked. *Able to engineer different types of animals. And under the dome there had been an illegal attempt to . . .*

"You're thinking about the Martian koalas, aren't you?" Susan said. Her pale cheeks began to flush. "I wasn't part of that project. And I was just as angry as anyone about the genetic manipulation of those animals. If you're going to use this article to accuse me of it, maybe we should stop this little interview right now."

"I'm not accusing you," I said. "I was just thinking about the koalas. How could I not? But—" I was stuck.

"But the article will be much better if readers see how angry you were about it," Ashley said to her. "As a genetic scientist and as a person."

Susan relaxed.

Good save, Ashley, I thought. I also realized that I really *did* want to write this article. It would be interesting, getting the different opinions of people on the ship. It was too bad that a possible hidden bomb and an onboard traitor were the other reasons for writing it.

"So 13 years of work, just to get to Mars . . . ," Ashley prompted the scientist. "And a eight-month trip across the middle of the solar system to get there. Do you think it was worth it?"

Susan nodded. "Every minute. Not just the science part. To be able to watch sunrises and sunsets on a different planet? To walk on the Martian sand and wonder about the universe? Incredible. And the bonus was that I got to work so hard on the genetic stuff too," she said, her voice growing louder and more enthusiastic.

"But you only stayed for one three-year shift," I said, almost without thinking. "Most scientists stay a lot longer after putting in all that effort to get there. And if you loved it so much, why leave?"

Susan shrank into herself, and her face became stone-cold. Grabbing her e-book, she tucked it under her arm. "Obviously this is a real interview. Just like most of the media on Earth. Rude. I've had enough." Without saying good-bye, she yanked at a handhold. It threw her forward toward the hatch, and she barely ducked in time to make it through.

"Really know how to charm them, don't you?" Ashley said, hand on her hip in her traditionally annoyed pose.

I tried a weak grin. "You still like me, right?"

"Humph."

"Come on. She's hiding something. Why would she suddenly leave Mars?"

"Humph."

Obviously Ashley didn't have an answer to that.

Which is what worried me the most.

CHAPTER 9

I floated into the computer control center. Aside from the navigation cone, it was the most important part of the ship. Dad explained it to me this way. If the *Moon Racer* was like a human body, the computer control center was the brain of the ship and the navigation cone, as it operated the movement of the ship, was the arms and legs that responded to the brain. With one slight difference. Since the pilot was the head commander in space, the navigational system—which depended on the computer control center—only worked after the pilot keyed in his password.

Other than this override from the navigational system, the computer control center monitored air, heating, communications, electrical, and all the dozens of other miniature systems that made life possible on the ship.

For such a crucial center, it didn't look like much. There was a mainframe computer attached to the wall, with a monitor in front and another monitor to the side. On the opposite wall, a second and third computer, each with a monitor, served as emergency backups. A straight-backed chair faced the main computer. That was it. All was lit by the soft white glow of the recessed argon tubes.

Lance Evenson sat in front of the computer, his big shoulders blocking most of the screen.

He wasn't alone. Luke Daab, tool belt strapped to his waist, had a couple of computer wires in his hand. Beside the mainframe, he'd taken off some wall panels. The mess of different-colored wires looked like a tangle of snakes. So close to Lance, Luke looked even smaller and more shrunken than usual.

I coughed discreetly to let them both know I had entered the room.

Luke glanced at me, then away with his usual shyness.

Lance turned and frowned at me. "What is it," he demanded. Not a question. But an almost angry statement.

"Um, Ashley and I are doing interviews for an article we want to write for people on Earth," I said. I didn't think Lance would agree to it, but I had to try. "We're wondering if you—"

"Not a chance," Lance snarled. "Trouble with too many people is that they don't mind their own business. Including you." He shifted and faced his computer monitor.

Blips and lines danced with random movement on what little of the screen I could see past his massive body.

I coughed again.

"What is it," Lance said in his same angry tone, not bothering to look away from the computer.

I had two reasons for being here. One was to make sure Lance was in the computer room and wouldn't find Ashley and me at the air vent in the corridor near his bunk. And the other reason was just as important.

"I'm expecting an e-mail from Rawling," I said. "But it hasn't shown up on my comp-board."

"We're 40 million miles from Mars," Lance growled, still watching the computer. "These things take time."

"I sent it late last night," I said. "I'm pretty sure he would have replied by now. Is there any chance it's somewhere on the mainframe?"

"Are you accusing me of keeping your private mail?"

"N-no . . . ," I stuttered. "Not at all. I'm just wondering—"

"That's another one of your problems," Lance said. "You wonder too much. I'll look into it. Now go away."

As I grabbed a handhold and prepared to push off, I noticed Luke Daab looking at me. Sadness seemed to fill his tiny, wrinkled face.

Then I realized something that made me feel guilty. I had totally ignored him. Like always. Like most people did, because he was a glorified janitor, almost invisible as he did the maintenance duties no one else wanted to do.

"Mr. Daab," I said, "would you be able to find time for an interview?"

"Yes," he said, suddenly smiling. "Thank you very much!"

In one way I felt better for asking him. And in another his eagerness made me feel even worse for first ignoring him. "How about this afternoon?" I said, hiding my guilt.

"Great," he said.

"That's great with me," I said as I pushed away and floated out of the computer control center.

It *was* great. By then Ashley and I would have had a chance to explore behind the vent in Lance's bunk. And maybe by then, we would have proved the chief computer technician was guilty of a lot more than just a bad temper.

CHAPTER 10

"Ready?" Ashley asked.

"Ready," I said.

"Checklist," she said.

On my back in the robot lab, I was strapped to the bed so that I couldn't move and accidentally break the connection between the antenna plug in my spine and the receiver across the room.

"One," I said, "no robot contact with any electrical sources."

My spinal nerves were attached to the plug. Any electrical current going into or through the robot would scramble the X-ray waves so badly that the signals reaching my brain would do serious damage.

"Two," I said, "I will disengage instantly at the first warning of any damage to the robot's computer drive."

My brain circuits worked so closely with the computer circuits that any harm to the computer would spill over to harm my brain.

"Last," I asked Ashley, "is the robot battery at full power?"

"Yes. And unplugged from the electrical source that charges it."

"I'm ready," I said.

"Let's go, then." Ashley placed a soundproof headset on my ears. The fewer distractions to reach my brain in my real body, the better.

It was dark and silent while I waited for a sensation that had become familiar and beautiful for me. The sensation of entering the robot computer.

My wait did not take long. Soon I began to fall off a high, invisible cliff into a deep, invisible hole.

I kept falling and falling and falling. . . .

Halfway across the spaceship, tiny video lenses opened on the head of a robot smaller than an ant.

Those lenses translated light patterns into a digital code, which was beamed by X-ray waves into the computer that was attached to my body through the spinal wiring. The digital code retranslated in my own brain, just like light patterns that entered my own eyes. I saw what the ant-bot saw—a huge tunnel that looked about a mile across, striped with shadows from the light that came through the slits of the air-vent cover behind it.

The tunnel wasn't that wide, of course. But from the ant-bot's perspective, everything seemed monstrous. Except for the splinter of plastic from a broken DVD-gigarom cover in its left hand.

Earlier Ashley and I had found the vent cover at the closest entry point to the vent that led into Lance's bunk. We had taken the cover off and had attached the ant-bot—armed with its splinter of plastic—to the inside of the vent so it wouldn't float away until we were ready.

Which was now.

In my own mind I gave a command for the ant-bot's right hand to let go of the inside of the vent cover. Immediately the flow of air spun the ant-bot farther into the vent.

Without the force of gravity, the ant-bot bounced and danced along the river of moving air like a speck of dust. I brought the right hand over to grip the splinter of plastic. I held the tiny spear of plastic crossways in front of me like a sail and waited for the air to take me to my destination.

The light that had reached the inside of the vent through the cover fell behind me, and darkness overwhelmed the ant-bot.

It was an eerie sensation of nothingness. No light. No sound. No gravity. And because I saw and heard nothing through the robot's video or audio, there was nothing to indicate that I was still moving. For all I could tell, I would be held by this darkness forever. I told myself otherwise and waited as patiently as I could.

With nothing to help my senses understand my surroundings, time stretched far too slowly. I was almost ready to believe that I was stuck forever in the darkness when the first dim light reached the ant-bot's video lenses. It came from Lance's bunk.

With the new stripes of that light growing brighter, I tried to orient the ant-bot so it faced the vent directly. It was impossible. The air tumbled the ant-bot in unpredictable directions.

The air-vent cover loomed larger and larger so that it looked like the face of a giant cliff as the ant-bot swept into it.

The slits of the cover were so big that the ant-bot could be sucked through it with the passing air. That's another reason why I held the splinter of plastic. Like a crossbeam, the plastic slammed into the vent and held the ant-bot in place.

I gripped the edge of the nearest vent cover slit and slowly released the ant-bot's right hand from the plastic. Once it was firmly attached, I was able to direct one of the video lenses to look back in the direction I had just traveled.

It took a couple of seconds to make sense of what I saw in the striped shadows of the air-vent slits. Especially because everything seemed so gigantic from the view of the ant-bot.

But then I realized what Lance was hiding. It wasn't in his bunk. It was here in the air vent.

A DVD-gigarom. Taped to the surface of the vent.

CHAPTER 11

"Where were you born?" I asked Luke Daab. "How big was your family? When did you start dreaming of going to Mars?"

We were the only two in the entertainment cluster. A giant screen filled one wall. The ship had hundreds of movies in DVD-gigarom format. Eight months was a long time to travel, and the 3-D movies really helped ease the boredom.

"Slow down. Slow down," he said with a shy smile. "I can't think that fast."

"Where were you born?" It was a good thing I had a list of prepared questions. My heart was not really in this interview. I was worried about what might happen to the ant-bot. And more worried about what Lance had hidden behind the vent in his bunk area. I was only here because I had agreed to meet Luke at this time and because Dad was too busy to see me right now.

"Key West." Luke scratched his face. "It's at the southern tip of Florida."

"Near Cuba," I added, thinking of my geography lessons.

"Near Cuba," he confirmed. "But remember, when I grew up, Cuba still wasn't one of the states of America. And shortly after it joined, the United States led the way for a world-federated government. Things have really changed since I was your age."

"Sounds like you miss it," I said without thinking. I had my list of questions to go through, and I should have stuck with it so this interview would end as quickly as possible. I had lots to do—as soon as Dad was finished with his computer check. Strange glitches had been showing up, and they were driving him crazy.

"When I was a kid," Luke said, his face twisting, "we had freedom. I could fish when and where I wanted. Sail across the water without a satellite camera filming me. My family could go on vacation without reporting it to the government first. There were no microchips to track everything a person did."

"From what I understand," I said cautiously, "people haven't lost much freedom and for that small loss of freedom have gained a lot of security. They—"

"You don't know what it was like! You haven't spent any time on Earth, but you still buy the arguments about a controlled economy and lack of crime!"

My eyes must have opened wide in surprise at his outburst. It seemed so unlike the Luke I'd seen quietly move about the spaceship for the past seven-plus months.

"Sorry," he said, the shy smile back in place. "That probably answers another one of your questions. Why I wanted to go to Mars. I thought a planet with no people on it might be a place of freedom."

"And . . . ?"

"You can call me a maintenance engineer in your article—" he smiled sadly—"but no matter what job title I get, I'm still a janitor. And janitors don't get treated much differently on Mars than they do on Earth. I didn't get much of a chance to see the planet."

"Oh."

"Don't get me wrong. It was still worth it. I was there when the dome was built, and this is my first trip back to Earth. If I hadn't liked it, I would have applied to come back much earlier."

"I guess 15 years on Mars was long enough. . . ." This was leading me to the one question Ashley and I wanted everyone to answer: Why they were going back to Earth. What reason they had for being on this ship with Blaine Steven and Dr. Jordan. If it seemed like they didn't have a good reason, it might be the first hint that something wasn't right.

"Maybe not," Luke answered. "But my father is really, really ill. I decided if I didn't go back now, I wouldn't have a chance to help my mother. As you can imagine, they are both very old."

I scanned the rest of my questions. There were four left, but I was itching to get to Dad and tell him what I knew. Luke had already answered the most important question about his reason for leaving Mars.

"Thanks, Mr. Daab," I said. "That really helps."

"That's it?"

I nodded. "That's it."

"Just as well," he said. "I have lots to do."

The sad part was that I think he knew I just wanted to get out of there. And even sadder, I think he expected it because he was a janitor.

I tried not to think about it anymore as I looked for Dad to tell him my news.

CHAPTER 12

"Let me get this straight," Dad said sternly. "You made an unauthorized use of the ant-bot and invaded the privacy of one of the members of the ship? Then you left the ant-bot—worth 15 billion dollars of technological research—attached to the inside of the air-vent cover in his bunk?"

I squirmed. A person wouldn't think that weightlessness would ever be uncomfortable, but even floating in midair I couldn't find a position that felt right. "I thought that if I found something that—"

"That the results would justify whatever way you did it?"

By the coldness in Dad's voice, I knew I was wrong to think *yes*. Even more, I was wrong not to consult him, as pilot, first. "Ashley and I didn't invade his privacy," I said

AMBUSH

201

quietly, trying to find a way to defend myself. "We didn't spy on him. We just went into the place where you had wanted me to vacuum earlier to search for the same thing. Remember? You asked us to look for whatever might be behind the vent covers in any of the bunks."

Dad sat on his pilot's chair. He had swiveled it away from the controls of the navigation cone as I'd entered. The black, star-studded sky, visible through the clear shell of the navigation cone, framed his broad shoulders. His eyes bored into mine.

"Earlier, you were doing it under the pilot's express directions. Now without the pilot's authorization, you have, by government law and by military ship regulations, engaged in a criminal act of utmost seriousness." The coldness did not leave his voice. "Furthermore, now that I have knowledge of your crime, I must take action against you. If not, again by government law and by military ship regulations, I too am guilty of this serious crime. Regardless of your intentions, any court-martial assembly would have no choice but to strip me of my pilot's license and possibly sentence me to jail time."

I closed my eyes as all of this sank in. To me, it had been a good solution to helping Dad solve the ship's crisis—without getting anyone else involved. I'd never dreamed I'd cause so much trouble.

"Now let me speak to you as a father, not the pilot," Dad said with a sigh.

I opened my eyes as the coldness left his voice.

He put a hand on my shoulder. "Tyce," he said gently, "you've placed me in a very difficult position. I'm not afraid to risk my career as a pilot. You're far more important to me than that. But to protect you, I would have to break my oath as a pilot. I would have to live a lie, and I can't live that way. . . ." He let his voice trail off into silence as he looked away from me. "Yet to do what the law and my oath require of me will hurt you more than I can bear."

I could think of no reply.

"Tell me," Dad said, still staring off into the emptiness of the solar system. "Did you find something that threatens the safety of the ship and passengers? some sort of explosive? anything like that?"

"No," I said. "But—"

"Stop there!"

I did.

"I don't want to hear what you found."

"But . . ."

A long, long silence followed before he began again. "By the pilot's code, the safety of ship and passengers takes priority over any other matter. I could make a case in military court for protecting you and acting on your information if we faced a threat. Otherwise . . ."

Again Dad sighed. He turned and faced me. "I have no choice." He picked up a cordless microphone from the console of the controls. Putting it to his mouth, he pushed a button on the side of it. He spoke quietly, entering the date and time into the audio log of the computer.

"Captain's report," he continued. "This is a formal report of a privacy violation enacted by passenger Tyce Sanders against chief computer technician Lance Evenson. As this is a first-time offense by said passenger, he is placed on a two-week probationary period. He is also instructed to make a formal apology to Lance Evenson within the next 24 hours."

Twenty-four hours? That was strange. If it was as serious as Dad said, why wouldn't he make me apologize immediately?

Dad clicked off the microphone and set it aside.

"I'm sorry," I said, hanging my head.

"Me too," he said. "The worst of it is that it sounds like I should know what you found."

"Yes, sir."

"But as it stands right now, if you told me, I would not be able to act upon illegally obtained information. I can only act if there is danger to the ship and passengers or if it was obtained by direct orders from the pilot."

"Yes, sir."

"Tyce, the rules and regulations of space travel have been set up to safeguard passengers. But rules and regulations are black-and-white. They can never be perfect and can never anticipate every situation. Nor can they perfectly deal with gray situations like this."

"Yes, sir."

"You understand that since you are on probation, if you violate any other rules of space travel, I must lock you in your bunk for the duration of the trip."

"Yes, sir."

"Having said that, I now give you a direct order to do your best to deliver me information that has been found in such a way that no court could dispute the legality with which it has been obtained."

"Sir?"

Dad looked at his watch, then smiled at me. "The clock is ticking, Son. In 23 hours and 56 minutes, by direct and recorded orders from the pilot of this ship, you are going to have to explain to Lance Evenson what you did and apologize for your actions."

"Sir?"

"Much as I didn't want to, I first had to address what you did by strictly following regulations, especially if any of this comes to trial. But my first priority as captain is to get this ship to Earth, and I will now move past the regulations, which don't cover a situation like this. What I'm telling you is that you now have 23 hours, 55 minutes, and 35 seconds to undo your mistake and find a way to get me the information you feel is vital to the continued operation of this ship. When we arrive on Earth, I will report everything. Including my instructions to you. If my handling of this situation is wrong, I intend to share whatever punishment you might receive."

CHAPTER 13

From: "Rawling McTigre" <mctigrer@marsdome.ss>
To: "Tyce Sanders" <sanderst@marsdome.ss>
Sent: 03.06.2040, 11:39 a.m.
Subject: Re: questions

Tyce,

Sorry I don't have anything to tell you at this point. If I learn anything that will be helpful, I'll let you know as soon as possible.

Rawling

I stared at my comp-board screen and reread the message three times. I'd finally received the e-mail from Rawling, but I had hoped for a lot more. *Where's the background information* on the passengers? Doesn't Rawling understand it's important enough that we need it, no matter how busy he is?

I read it again, as if that would help. Which it didn't.

Is Rawling mad at me? Normally he ended all his e-mails to me by signing off with "carpe diem, Rawls." He'd once told me that *carpe diem* was Latin for "seize the day." It was the motto he tried to live by. He said that it was important to live bravely, and he hoped I would always remember that.

Why hadn't he reminded me to seize the day like he did in all his other e-mails? I also noticed the time the e-mail had been sent. An hour after I had asked Lance about it. Which was 12 hours after I'd sent the first e-mail to Rawling.

Weird. I expected that Rawling would have replied much quicker.

I thought about it awhile, then hit Reply and began to keyboard a message in return.

From: "Tyce Sanders" <sanderst@marsdome.ss>
To: "Rawling McTigre" <mctigrer@marsdome.ss>
Sent: 03.06.2040, 2:51 p.m.
Subject: Re: questions

Rawling,

Thanks for getting back to me. I know you are doing your best. I think we have a little time before it absolutely becomes crucial. In the meantime, take care of your sore

elbow. Remember, you're no longer the young hockey player
of your university days that I've heard so much about.

    Tyce

I hit Send and smiled grimly. His reply to this message
would tell me a lot of what I needed to know.

While I waited, I had other questions to ask of someone else.

I opened up a word processing file on my comp-board
and let my fingers fly across the keyboard.

Even as I concentrated on the words popping up on the
screen, I was too aware of how little time I had left before my
next appointment.

"Hello," I said to the man hooked to the wall by cable. I had
tucked my comp-board under my arm. "Yesterday you said
you wanted to talk. So I'm here."

"Good," Steven replied. "Let's talk about God. You'd be
surprised at how interested I am."

He was right. I would be surprised—if he really meant
it. Frankly, after all the things Steven had done, I'd written
him off a long time ago. Mom always talked about God being
so big that no one was ever beyond his reach, but sometimes
it was hard for me to believe that. Especially around people
like Blaine Steven and Dr. Jordan.

Somehow I still assumed that his faith question had been an excuse to talk for the benefit of whoever might be listening in on our conversation.

"Tell me," he said. "If something happened to the *Moon Racer* and I died in the next two weeks, why would God ever want anything to do with me? I mean, I haven't exactly been the best person in the world."

I laughed. "Neither have I."

Steven looked surprised. "You haven't tried to kill anyone or take over the Mars Dome or . . ."

I repeated how Mom had explained it to me: "If a person had to jump from Earth to the moon, would it make any difference if he could jump six inches off the ground or six feet? Either way, he doesn't have a chance."

"True, but what does this have to do with my question?"

"Nobody can make himself perfect enough to get to God," I said. "No matter what you've done compared to what I have or haven't done, neither of us can jump to the moon."

"And?"

"It's the same with God. We can't get to him by ourselves. We need his help. But he's waiting for us—to reach for him. Then he forgives us and gives us love, instead of what we really deserve."

I could see Steven was listening. I was really glad that Mom and I had had talks about this.

"I know my mom and dad love me," I continued. "But if

I decided I wanted to have nothing to do with them for the rest of my life, no amount of their love could make me return to them. All they could do is wait for me to want them in my life again. And as soon as I reached out to them, they would welcome me back with open arms."

"Are you saying it's the same with God?" he said, looking intrigued.

"If you pretend he doesn't exist—just like if I pretended my parents don't exist—how can he ever be part of your life? Or you part of him?"

Steven seemed puzzled. "That gives me a lot to think about." He let out a deep breath and pointed at my comp-board.

Wordlessly I opened up my comp-board and fired up the word processing program. When the screen showed my questions, I carefully reached across the space between us and handed it to him.

He scanned the screen and nodded.

"Good-bye," I said. "I'll probably be back in an hour. If you'd like to talk some more."

"That would be fine," Steven said. He didn't lift his head. He had already begun to type.

CHAPTER 14

Every time I tried to move quickly from handhold to hand-hold, I thought of the old movie about Tarzan of the jungle, swinging through the vines. I resisted the urge to make a jungle noise as I sped toward the simulation center, exactly halfway across the ship. Ashley was waiting for me, and I had an idea I wanted to share with her.

As I followed the curve of the corridor's circle, the light seemed dimmer. Seconds later I saw why as I almost hit Luke. He was hanging in midair in the center of the corridor, with a lighting panel floating beside him. One argon tube hung beside the panel. He had another tube in his hand and was replacing the first one. A few scattered tools hung in the air nearby.

"Hey, Mr. Daab," I said. As I pushed quickly to one side

I had a glimpse of the wiring in the corridor's ceiling. I narrowly missed him and his tools as I aimed for the corridor wall directly beside him. When I hit the wall, I pushed off again toward the center. It put me right back at the handholds on the opposite side of him. I reached for the next handhold and kept going. I called over my shoulder, "See you later!"

"Good-bye, Tyce," he said. "Be careful!"

Careful? From my wheelchair all my life I had watched people walk or run past me on strong, healthy legs. To me this was the closest I would ever get to any kind of real freedom outside of my wheelchair. It was too much fun for me to worry about being careful.

A much darker thought hit me as I continued to swing from handhold to handhold.

If the spaceship never made it to Earth, how much would it matter if I was careful or not?

"What's that?" Ashley asked once I reached our computer station. She had her own comp-board in front of her, screen flipped open.

"Regulation jumpsuit," I said. I had folded the blue jumpsuit across my right arm. "Picked it up on the way here." I decided I wouldn't tell Ashley about my run-in with Dad. She and I had enough other things to think about.

"I know it's a jumpsuit. *Why* do you have it?"

"If you wanted to know why, you should have asked that in the first place."

"Tyce!" She flashed her dark eyes at me.

"Ashley!" I said, imitating her.

She sighed and shook her head. "I guess I'll be the mature one and move right along to the serious business and tell you about the rest of the interviews."

"Sure," I said, still grinning. I was in a great mood. And she would find out why very soon.

"I managed to speak to everyone else," Ashley said. "As it turns out, I didn't discover anything unusual. But I know why Susan Fielding is going back to Earth so soon."

"Oh?" With my right hand, I grabbed the sleeve of the jumpsuit near the shoulder. With my left hand, I held the rest of the jumpsuit.

"She needs some medical checkups. I couldn't find out exactly what kind, but that's what Jack Tripp was able to tell me when I interviewed him. And there doesn't seem to be anything strange in what he told me about himself. What do you think we should do next since—?"

I yanked as hard as I could. With a loud rip, the sleeve began to separate from the rest of the jumpsuit.

"What are you doing?" Ashley asked.

"Ripping off a sleeve."

"I can see that. But *why* are you—?"

"If you wanted to know why, you should have asked that in the first place."

"Aaaaaarghh."

I grinned again. Yes, I was in a good mood. I knew exactly how we were going to prove Lance Evenson was behind this.

I plucked at the loosened material in my hands. "When I'm finished with this, you'll be ready to call me a genius."

I explained as I continued to unravel threads from the jumpsuit.

And she, too, began to smile.

CHAPTER 15

Half an hour later, Ashley and I returned to the robot lab. Much as I wanted to rush through the checklist process, Ashley forced us to go slowly.

Finally I was strapped in place, in darkness and silence.

Then, as always, came the sensation of falling . . . falling . . . .

My return to sight brought the striped shadows of the air-vent cover of Lance Evenson's bunk. Those shadows fell on the DVD-gigarom that was taped to the inside of the vent.

I brought one of the ant-bot arms up in front of me. I waggled it, simply because I never got tired of working a robot through the nerve impulses sent by my brain. Incredible as the ant-bot's engineering might be, I didn't intend to try to move the disc or carry it.

No, even here in the weightlessness of outer space, that would take something else.

I didn't have to wait long.

Just as the air current had earlier sent the ant-bot floating down here to the vent cover, it now brought something else.

Thread.

Or, more precisely, one thread tied to another thread tied to another and another and another. I had taken threads from the jumpsuit and knotted them to form a long, long single thread. Then, to make sure the air current would bring the thread down the vent, I had tied one end to a small square of paper.

Through the video lens of the ant-bot, I watched that small square approach like a sail ahead of a breeze in one of the pirate movies I loved to watch. The thread trailing it was invisible in the darkness of the vent shaft. But when the paper reached the vent cover, I was easily able to grab the piece of thread in the tiny robot hand. I pulled it loose from the piece of paper.

The only tricky part would come next.

Because of the lack of gravity, I could not simply let go of the vent cover and expect to drop. I would have to launch the ant-bot in the direction of the disc.

Seconds later I made the leap. Although I covered only

about six inches, to the ant-bot it was like a jump that covered five football fields.

As the ant-bot floated through the air, I tied one end of the thread around the ant-bot's other arm. Though it was just a thread of fabric, it seemed like a rope. When I landed, I had the rope securely lashed. Then both of the ant-bot's arms were free for use.

There wasn't much surface on the disc small enough for the ant-bot to actually get a grip on it. But it didn't matter. I had aimed my jump well enough to land beside the single strand of tape that held the disc against the inside surface of the vent.

First I pried a small part of the edge of the tape off the disc. I unwrapped the thread from the ant-bot arm and pushed it against the sticky underside of the tape. I tugged. It wasn't much of a tug. A human hand would have easily ripped the thread loose. But the ant-bot didn't have that kind of strength, and the thread remained in place.

Then I began the longer task of cutting the tape where it joined between the disc and the vent.

The ant-bot hands were tiny, and the tape seemed as thick as a slice of bread might look to human eyes. But since ant-bot hands were made of titanium, it was easy to claw through the tape.

When I finished cutting the tape on both sides of the disc, I had one last task.

I pulled on the thread to get a little slack. I looped it a couple of times around the ant-bot's neck. Then in my mind I shouted, *"Stop!"*

Instantly I woke up back in the robot lab.

Ashley and I stood in the corridor with a vent cover hanging beside us.

She held a piece of thread in her hands and slowly pulled.

Because there was no gravity, I knew she didn't feel the weight of the disc on the other end of the thread. But she kept pulling, trusting that the ant-bot had done the job properly.

As she kept reeling in thread, the disc appeared. She grabbed it with her hand and gave it to me.

I loosened the thread where the ant-bot had stuck it to the tape on the disc. Hanging from the thread was the tiny body of the ant-bot.

"Mission accomplished." I grinned. "One disc. And one recovered ant-bot."

"You mean step one accomplished," she corrected me. "Now we need to find out what's on the disc."

CHAPTER 16

"This is it." I waved my opened comp-board at Ashley. "In five minutes, we're going to have all the answers."

We were back in the entertainment cluster, alone. It had taken hardly any time to retrieve my comp-board from Blaine Steven.

"How can you know that? You haven't even opened the disc yet."

"I'm not talking about just the disc." It was in the front pocket of my jumpsuit. All I needed to do was fit it into the discport on the right-hand side of the comp-board, and we'd find out what was on it. But first the other information. "Blaine Steven had my comp-board for the last hour. He—"

"Blaine Steven? You let him access your computer?"

I explained why. "See this," I said as I clicked on the file with my questions for him. The words sprang into shape on my screen. I leaned over to let Ashley share my view of it. "I put in the questions and he's given the answers."

I read it silently with her.

> Why do you think Dr. Jordan and this mastermind person want you dead?

> Because I know how the Terratakers work. I know too much about them. I can expose them and testify against them. They don't care whether I ever intend to do anything against them. They will get rid of me simply because it is a safe thing to do. I was never afraid of them when I was on Mars because they needed me when I was director. But as I get closer to Earth, I am more afraid. Especially because I hear Dr. Jordan having conversations in the bunk beside me. I can't hear the words; I just know that someone is visiting him late at night. The mastermind. I know that if they wanted me to continue to be part of the rebels, the mastermind would come to my bunk too. But they are leaving me alone.

> Why would they want everyone else on the ship dead?

Because it is safer for them. If they escape the *Moon Racer*, they will be picked up by a rebel space shuttle. Dr. Jordan won't be arrested then. The mastermind will be able to disappear into the underworld of the Terratakers, who are spread across the world. And if they are the only survivors, no one will ever be able to contradict them.

Why should I believe anything you tell me?

If you don't believe me now, you will when something starts going wrong with the *Moon Racer*. If it isn't an explosive device, which is my first guess, it will be something else. I hope I'm wrong about all of this. If we make it to Earth safely, then you can laugh at me as the military officials arrest me.

Why should Dad or I help you?

I have many, many secrets that can help the World United Federation defeat the rebels before they find a way to start a new world war. That is their goal. Once a war begins and the confederation of countries splits up, they can take advantage of the confusion and of the weaker countries.

I was about to comment when, *Bing!* The tinny noise from my comp-board jolted me away from the words on the screen.

My e-mail announcement. Mail had just arrived.

"Hang on," I said to Ashley. I clicked a few buttons on the keyboard to open my e-mail. "Hopefully it's from Rawling. That will give us even more information."

The e-mail symbol jumped into the foreground of the screen, leaving my question-and-answer interview with Blaine Steven in the background.

I double-clicked to open the new e-mail.

"Yep," I said. "Rawling."

From: "Rawling McTigre" <mctigrer@marsdome.ss>
To: "Tyce Sanders" <sanderst@marsdome.ss>
Sent: 03.06.2040, 4:13 p.m.
Subject: Re: questions

Tyce,

I still don't have anything to tell you that might be of help. I'll keep looking, however, and get to you immediately if I learn anything.

   Rawling

P.S. The elbow is getting better. I know it hurts me a lot less than it hurt other people in my old hockey days on Earth!

"I knew it!" I pointed at the screen. "I just knew it!"

"If you get any more excited, you'll start to drool." Ashley frowned. "And I don't see much to get excited about."

"He normally signs off differently." I told Ashley about how Rawling always ended his e-mails to me with "carpe diem, Rawls."

"So he forgot," Ashley said. "He *is* director of the Mars Dome. Plus, he's got to be worried about this spaceship. With everything else happening on Mars . . ."

"He's also taking a lot longer than usual to reply."

"Because he's taking all that time to try to find answers for you."

I shook my head. "The Rawling I know would fire off an immediate e-mail explaining that it might take a while to get what he needs."

"The Rawling you know? Meaning this Rawling is—"

"Someone else." I pointed at the P.S. of the e-mail and read it out loud. "'The elbow is getting better. I know it hurts me a lot less than it hurt other people in my old hockey days on Earth!'"

"Even I understand what he means," Ashley said, still unimpressed at my excitement. "In hockey, players sometimes elbow other players."

"Not Rawling. He didn't play hockey in his university days. He played football."

Ashley's eyes widened as she began to understand.

"Look at my original e-mail to him."

She reread it with me. *"Remember, you're no longer the young hockey player of your university days that I've heard so much about."*

"I wrote that because I knew he was a quarterback. If it was Rawling who received the message and if it was Rawling who wrote back, he would have corrected me, not agreed with me!"

"Someone else is intercepting your e-mail?"

"Who has control of the computers on board this ship?"

"Lance Evenson!" Ashley was getting as excited as I was. "The same guy who hid a disc."

"Yes. The same guy who—" I hit my head. "No, no, no!" I began to fumble with my comp-board.

"Tyce?" Ashley asked.

I didn't take the time to answer. I frantically clawed at a small compartment on the underside of my keyboard. I needed to pull out the battery and shut down my computer.

In front of our eyes, the words on the comp-board screen were beginning to dissolve.

The same person who had intercepted my e-mail was logged on to my computer through the mainframe. And trying to destroy all the information on it!

CHAPTER 17

"Dad!" I shouted. "Dad!"

I wasn't even all the way down the tube that led to the navigation cone. "Dad! Are you there!"

If he wasn't in front of his controls, I didn't want to waste time going all the way down and then back up.

"Yes, I'm here, Tyce." His calm voice helped me relax. He would know what to do. And how to do it.

I dropped into the navigation cone. Dad spun around in his chair. His face was tired.

"I think I have the answers you need," I said.

"Good, because I don't seem to be getting anywhere by myself. What have you got?"

"A quick quiz."

"Ready."

"What," I asked, "do all of these have in common: ship controls, escape pod controls, e-mail, networks, and Lance Evenson?"

I answered it for him. "Mainframe computer. All of the commands you give through the controls here are handled by the mainframe. Right? Same with everything else. In fact, just about every single thing on this ship is controlled through the mainframe. And who handles the mainframe? Lance Evenson."

"He doesn't have all the passwords. Without them, he can't override the pilot controls."

"Say somehow he did. Then won't you agree he's the one person who would have complete control of the ship? the one person who could activate an escape pod as soon as he needs it?"

"Well . . ."

"Follow me," I said. "And hopefully I can prove it."

He rose from his pilot's chair.

"Dad, you'd better unlock your neuron gun for this."

We met Ashley back at the entertainment cluster. She had her own comp-board open on her lap.

"Did it work?" I asked her.

She nodded. "I plugged the port on the back of the comp-board by pressing my finger against it, just like you suggested."

"Good," I said. With my comp-board out of commission, Ashley had gone to get hers while I found Dad. "And did you find what I thought you'd find on Lance's disc?"

Ashley nodded again. "A security override program. If I'm reading it correctly, it looks like I can get anywhere inside the mainframe with it."

"Dad?" I said softly.

"This is serious. But it still doesn't explain how someone on the mainframe can interfere with the pilot controls. My password is only registered on Earth, with the military, and it's under the tightest security you could imagine. It would only be given out in an emergency situation if someone else had to take over this ship."

"There's more on this disc," Ashley said. She held out the comp-board screen.

Dad looked over my shoulder. When he saw the contents of the disc, he whistled. "Look at the labels on those files! Communication files. E-mail files. Reports and documents. It's like years of information stolen from the Mars Dome computer!"

"How much would that be worth on Earth?" I asked. "All that information? Sold to the wrong people, like the rebels?"

Dad shook his head. "Enough, I guess, that whoever owned this disc would find it worthwhile to let everyone else on the ship die. I just never thought it would be Lance."

Dad made his decision. "What we do next is take this disc to Lance. We'll see what he has to say about it."

Ashley and I followed.

I couldn't help but notice that as Dad led the way, he touched the neuron gun on his hip. As if he were making sure it was there and ready.

CHAPTER 18

"No," Lance said. He groaned. "That's my disc. But it's not me doing everything else."

Dad and Ashley and I had met him at the computer control center. Dad had not said much beyond a quiet hello before asking permission to insert the disc into the mainframe.

When the contents of the disc had appeared on the monitor in front of Lance, he'd covered his face with his hands.

To me, it was the action of a guilty man. I found it difficult to keep my mouth shut. But Dad was the pilot. Dad would handle this.

"You don't sound surprised to find out someone has been using the mainframe for all of this," Dad said. "You're saying someone else has?"

"I have nothing more to say." Lance folded his big arms

across his big chest. "Except that I have done nothing to threaten the safety of this ship."

"Prove it, then," Dad said, still quiet. "Open the log of your mainframe computer activities."

"All right," Lance said after several seconds of thought. He began to punch out a series of commands on his keyboard. "You'll see I'm innocent of that."

"But guilty of something else? Like possession of a master disc with a security override program? And with masses of highly confidential Mars Dome files?"

"I have nothing more to say in that regard. But I did nothing to threaten the safety of this ship. And if you look at the activity log . . ." Lance gasped. Lines of numbers showed brightly on the screen. "Impossible. Totally impossible. I look at this log at least three times a day, and I've never seen these numbers before."

"What?" Dad asked.

Lance touched the screen and followed a line of numbers. "Here. A command to unlock the prisoner's cable in bunk number five, just past midnight last night. Then to open the hatch to the corridor. And a command to seal it again two hours later. I . . . I . . . did not program this."

Bunk number five? That's Dr. Jordan's bunk. He's been out of his prison bunk for two hours?

"Let me get this straight," Dad said. "Someone released

Jordan last night. And then Jordan returned to the prison bunk."

So Blaine Steven has not been lying about a mastermind on board!

Lance scanned the lines. "And the night before. And the night before that. In fact, it looks like Jordan has come and gone at his convenience almost since the ship left Mars."

"Why would you do that?" Dad asked.

"It wasn't me. I can tell you that. The man gives me the creeps."

"You want me to believe that someone else on this ship actually controls the mainframe." Dad's voice grew louder.

Lance ignored him and continued to scan the lines of the computer activity log. "Here. Unauthorized log-on to a personal comp-board. ID code 0808."

ID code 0808. My comp-board! "What time?" I asked.

"More than once," Lance told me, reading the lines of code. "Including less than a half hour ago. Whoever logged on stole all the information on it and kept updating the new information you added."

That person knows about the secret conversations I was having with Blaine Steven!

"And here," Lance said, unaware of my anger and fear. "Disable commands to the escape pods. And here, commands that override the pilot controls."

That explains the malfunctions Dad had been fighting.

Lance looked at Dad with bewilderment. He had the face of a big kid, scared. "Wasn't me. I didn't do any of this!"

"Then who?"

"If I knew, I would tell you," Lance answered. "It could be anyone on this ship with a comp-board and the right security codes to access the mainframe."

"How? You don't let anyone into this computer room, do you?"

"I don't know how," Lance said in frustration.

"Think!" Dad said. "How would you do it?"

Lance shrugged. "I'd tap into a wire off the back of the mainframe and run that wire out somewhere in the ship. But not to my bunk, because it would be too easy to get caught. Instead, I'd run it to an infrared antenna that could be hidden anywhere and link from my comp-board that way. But you can't run that wire from this mainframe without time and access. Nobody has had either in this computer room."

He caught Dad's glare. "I know! I know! Then it really looks like I'm the one. But I'm not."

"I can order a search of all the comp-boards on the ship," Dad said. "That will prove you right. Or wrong. In the meantime, undo those commands. Get the escape pods in working condition. Most of all, give me complete control again of the navigation cone."

"If I can," Lance said. He had his finger on the screen, running it below one of the lines.

"If you can?"

"This code . . . I have to figure out the code before I can override it."

"Which means?"

"Whoever has been tapping into the mainframe has complete control. Without the computer that's been instructing the mainframe, it will be impossible to undo all the commands that came from it."

"Then we'll begin looking," Dad said grimly, "and I expect total cooperation from you."

Dad stared at Lance. Lance stared right back at him.

I looked beyond them at the computer screen. "Dad?"

The numbers on the screen began to dissolve. At the same time, the hatch door to the computer room began to close.

CHAPTER 19

Dad reacted first. He shoved off a handhold and made a mid-air dive for the hatch door. It shut squarely on his body, pinning him in the opening, with his legs inside the computer room and his upper body stuck in the corridor.

Normally a hatch door was sequenced by the computer to reopen if it hit any objects. This was a built-in safety feature to prevent exactly what had just happened.

I pushed toward him. "Dad? You all right?"

"Not good," Dad grunted from the other side. The hatch door pressed hard against his ribs. "Find something to jam in here so I can squeeze out. I don't know what's happening, but the last thing I want is us trapped in this room. Or unable to reenter once we're outside."

I looked behind me. There was nothing I could use. Just

the mainframe computer, the monitor, a desk, and the chair Lance was strapped on. The rest was bare walls and ceiling.

"Hurry, Tyce," Dad grunted. "I think the door has got my diaphragm. I can't breathe!"

Being trapped or not suddenly seemed a lot less important than saving Dad's life. I rushed back to the hatch. I wedged one hand against the edge of the open hatchway and the other against the partly closed door. I tried to pull them apart. I pulled so hard that my vision turned black and I saw little stars.

"I . . . can't!" I peered back at Lance, who was staring at me from his desk in front of the computer monitor. "Please . . . I need help!"

This was the moment. If Lance was really the mastermind and had lied when he told us it was someone else controlling the ship's computer, then he'd let my dad die.

I futilely tried to pull again. "Help!"

It seemed like he moved in slow motion, but finally Lance came toward me, with Ashley following.

Lance took over my position. This was the first time I was glad that he was such a big man.

I backed up and inspiration hit me. The ceiling panels!

I grabbed a handhold with my left hand. With my right, I yanked at a ceiling panel. It came loose. It was a square piece of plastic, about a foot wide and an inch thick. I didn't know if one would do it. I yanked another loose. Then a third.

I spun back toward the hatch. With all three tiles stacked together, I put the bottom into the opening first, beneath Dad's legs. The opening was less than a foot wide, however, and I could not wedge the top of the square into place.

Below where Dad was stuck in the hatch, Lance was straining hard, veins bulging in his neck as he struggled to slide open the hatch door. Above Dad, Ashley had braced herself by jamming her feet against the edge of the hatchway and pulling on the hatch with both hands. She was bent like a bow and screaming with effort.

Slowly the hatch door moved back. As Dad slipped out, I jammed the ceiling tiles in place.

Lance and Ashley let go of the hatch, and it slammed against the wedged tiles.

Dad pushed backward and let out a deep breath. "Good," he said, as the tiles held in place. "Now we're not trapped."

I let out my own sigh of relief.

Just then the spaceship jolted forward with sudden acceleration. All of us were hurled against the back wall.

"Is someone at the controls?" Dad shouted at Lance.

They both shoved themselves back toward the computer monitor.

Seconds later Lance gave us the answer we didn't want to hear. "Negative. Nobody is in the navigation cone," he answered as he read the monitor. "It looks like the computer has somehow been preprogrammed to do this. And the acceleration is continuing!"

As he finished speaking, the wailing sound of an alarm siren filled the ship.

My eyes met Dad's. We both knew that there was only one reason for that sound.

Someone had just begun the escape pod countdown.

CHAPTER 20

The corridor was strangely empty.

The siren wailed its piercing shriek to give notice that time was running out before the escape pod ejected. In the past few months, Dad had run the occasional drill—even during the night a couple of times—to prepare us for an emergency situation. Once the siren sounded there was less than three minutes to reach the pod.

But none of the ship's passengers had left their bunks to see what was happening.

Just as well.

We swung from handhold to handhold, moving as fast as we could down the corridor toward the escape pods. If the others had wandered out of their bunks into our path, it would have made for a disastrous collision.

The walls of the corridor seemed to blur in the confusion of our frantic scuttling. The noise gained in volume.

Finally we rounded the curve to reach the escape pods.

Just in time to see Dr. Jordan with Luke Daab.

They saw the three of us.

Luke's mouth moved like he was shouting for us. But his words were drowned out by the siren.

"Stop!" Dad yelled uselessly above the din of the siren. I could barely hear him myself, and I was right beside his shoulder. "Stop!" He pulled his neuron gun from his belt and aimed. "Stop!"

Dr. Jordan might not have been able to hear Dad, but he could see the gun. We were less than 20 feet away from him. He reacted by grabbing Luke in a choke hold and using him as a shield.

Dad fired the neuron gun. The discharge would stun all of the neuron pathways in both Dr. Jordan and Luke, hurting them both but not damaging either of them permanently.

Nothing happened.

Dr. Jordan grinned evilly at Dad, turning his round face into a pucker of satisfied smugness.

Then I understood. The neuron gun could only operate under two conditions. The fingerprints of the person holding the gun had to match the computer instructions in the neuron gun's microchip. And activation had to be permitted by the mainframe computer.

If Dr. Jordan was somehow controlling the mainframe, he would have also disabled the neuron gun.

Dad fired again. Then he must have realized the same thing I did.

I felt Ashley bump against me.

The three of us against Dr. Jordan. We still had a chance, even without the neuron gun. Four of us, if Luke could get out of the choke hold.

"Back away!" Dr. Jordan shouted. We were close enough that we could barely hear him above the siren. Light bounced off his round glasses, hiding his eyes from us. "I'll snap his neck like a chicken bone!"

To emphasize his threat, Dr. Jordan squeezed the choke hold harder with his right forearm and began to turn Luke's head with his left hand. Pain and fear filled the small janitor's face.

Dad stopped.

Dr. Jordan smiled coldly. "Good-bye! I know you've been looking for a bomb. Too bad you didn't think computer bomb, because the chain of events I started on your mainframe is going to be very interesting! Start putting on your sunscreen!"

With those final words, he pulled Luke into the escape pod. The hatch slid shut behind them.

And 20 seconds later the escape pod ejected from the ship.

CHAPTER 21

I stared at points of light through the clear wall of the navigation cone. Only in my imagination could I wonder if I saw sunlight gleaming off the escape pod. Even though only half an hour had passed, it was thousands of miles away.

"It doesn't make me feel better that I was right in my guess," Dad said. A blip on his monitor showed the location of the escape pod. "Jordan's using the momentum of the ship for a slingshot effect. Add our current speed to the speed of the pod's ejection from the ship, plus the burst of acceleration from its own fuel supply, and the escape pod has effectively doubled our speed. Which means they . . ."

It took Dad a few seconds to make his calculation. "They'll be in orbit range of Earth in 10 days. And we're not scheduled to arrive for almost three weeks."

"Wrong." Lance had dropped from the travel tube into the navigation cone.

"Wrong?" Dad repeated.

"Wrong," he said, frowning. "But let me give you all the good news first. That radio signal you want me to send ahead with news about his escape? Except for an emergency beacon, our mainframe won't permit any communications. In or out of the ship. It's part of the preprogramming that was coded into the mainframe without our authorization."

"That's the good news?" Dad said.

"Sure," Lance said in a voice heavy with sarcasm. "Plus the fact that I still can't break the computer code that has locked down all the hatches. Everyone is still stuck in their bunks with no access to food or water."

"Any more good news?"

"Unless you want to know that I found a wire from the mainframe to an infrared antenna in the ceiling panel half-way down the corridor. Which means whoever did the new programming had as much time as they wanted to make it foolproof. Which means I'm not sure I can break the new code soon enough. Unless I find the computer that wrote that code."

"Soon enough?"

Lance shook his head. "Sure. Now I get to tell you the bad news. Our ion engine is burning fuel at a tremendous rate. Remember the acceleration jolt we felt just before the siren went off?"

Dad nodded.

"Mainframe again. Instructing the engine to go into overdrive. Our engine is set at maximum, and every 30 minutes we're picking up speed at the rate of 1,000 miles an hour. By tomorrow, we'll be close to 50,000 miles an hour faster than we are now. With that much speed, we'll probably pass the escape pod before it's halfway to Earth."

Looking out through the navigation cone gave me no sense of the speed of our ship. Unlike on the surface of Mars—where the nearby boulders served as reference points and even 20 miles an hour seemed fast because of it—here in space the nearest reference points were billions of miles away. It took days to see any shift, so it never felt like we were moving.

"Lance, you've got to slow this down," Dad said. "With that kind of speed, hitting a pebble could blow us apart. And—" He stopped as his face suddenly went blank.

"Exactly," Lance said. "Getting blown apart might be the best we could hope for."

"What?" I asked. "If we don't hit anything, what can be so bad about reaching Earth's orbit so soon? We'll even beat Dr. Jordan there and be able to wait for him and save Luke."

"We'll reach Earth's orbit," Lance agreed. Quietly. "And then blow through it and past it."

"Tyce," Dad added, "at the beginning of a space journey like this, fuel is burned to accelerate us to maximum safe speed. Once we're at that speed, we coast with no friction to slow us down. Some fuel is burned in the middle for slight adjustments in the flight course. If the calculations are done right, there's enough fuel left at the end of the journey to put the engine in a reverse thrust and slow us down. That's space travel. Gradual acceleration. Followed by gradual deceleration. With just enough fuel loaded to take care of both."

Did that mean what I thought it meant?

Dad continued. "Our fuel margins are thin anyway. We build in about a 10 percent error rate. What's happening now is that every hour of fuel we burn puts us in double jeopardy. It's an extra hour of gained speed and one less hour of fuel to slow us down. Lance, have you done the rest of the calculations?"

"Yes. And that's the worst news I can deliver."

"I'd rather know it now," Dad said.

I wasn't sure if I wanted to hear it.

"If I can't find a way to break the programming code sometime in the next two hours," Lance told us, "we may have gained too much speed. Burning what remains of our fuel with the reverse thruster after that will only slow us down to a couple thousand miles per hour. And then no more fuel. There will be nothing left to bring us to a stop. And you know how it is in space. We'll just keep coasting at that speed."

At a couple thousand miles per hour. Forever?

"What if you can't break the programming code at all?" Dad asked.

"We continue accelerating until the fuel is gone. We pass the Earth at over 100,000 miles per hour. Headed straight toward the sun."

That's what Dr. Jordan meant when he told us to start putting on sunscreen. He knew exactly what had been planned.

Dad closed his eyes, then opened them. He spoke very calmly. "What you're saying is that in two hours, even if the computer lets us start communicating with anyone on Earth, there is no way any orbit shuttle would be able to catch or stop this ship as it flew past."

"That's exactly what I'm saying," Lance agreed. "We're only going to live as long as our food supplies last. Unless we hit the sun first."

CHAPTER 22

Diabolical.

That's the only way I can describe it.

I'm not even sure there is any point in writing any of this in my journal. After all, who will ever be able to read it when my comp-board and everything else on this ship burns down to a collection of atoms and molecules spewed out of the sun?

Or maybe we'll miss the sun and head to the outer reaches of the solar system, then beyond. Our ship will be lifeless, carrying only skeletons. And it's not likely that anyone would ever find this ghost ship and read my journal.

All because of that diabolical Dr. Jordan.

By getting into the mainframe, he had set

the ship's engine on maximum burn. If that wasn't enough, he blocked our communications systems so we couldn't radio for help or send a message explaining how he'd doomed the ship. And if that wasn't enough insurance to make sure no one lived, Dr. Jordan had the computer close down every hatch so everyone would be trapped in their bunks. Only because Dad had reacted quickly and instinctively did that final part of Dr. Jordan's plan fail. Well, at least with Dr. Jordan now escaped, I don't have to worry about someone logging on to my comp-board.

In the silence and privacy of my own bunk, I stopped keyboarding.

Almost two hours had passed since our discussion in the navigation cone. Long enough for Dad to manually break open every hatch door and let everyone out and tell them the bad news. And long enough for us to pass the point of no return. Now, even if Lance regained control of the mainframe, we didn't have enough fuel to bring the ship to a stop. Now, even if we could start the communications system, an SOS for help would do no good. We were traveling too fast for any military ship to rescue us.

SOS.

When I'd asked, Dad had explained that SOS meant

"save our souls," a plea from sinking ships when the ancient technology of wireless telegraph meant messages had to be sent by something called Morse code.

Save our souls.

Believe it or not, Blaine Steven, stuck behind with the rest of us, had actually started praying with Dad. Funny how the thought of death makes a person also think of God. Especially a person I'd assumed would never be faintly interested in God.

And Lance Evenson?

He'd told us the rest of the story behind the disc in his air vent. How from the beginning of his time on Mars he'd allowed an unknown someone access to the Mars Dome's mainframe. It had been ridiculously simple, he'd explained. All it took was giving that person the access code.

Why? Dad had asked.

Money, Lance had explained. Enough retirement money that when he returned to Earth, he would have no worries. He'd thought that taking all the information, including the security override program, with him on the disc would be insurance in case someone found out what he did and tried to blackmail him.

Who? Dad had asked.

That was just it, Lance had answered. He never knew. The money went into a bank account on Earth with regular payments that he could check with e-mail requests from

Mars. All Lance knew was that it had to be someone on Mars who had also been there from the beginning. And that this unknown person had access to a computer that tapped into the Mars Dome mainframe. Just like he'd done it on this spaceship.

I read from the beginning of what I had typed.

One sentence stuck out.

Well, at least with Dr. Jordan now escaped, I don't have to worry about someone logging on to my comp-board.

Why had I assumed I didn't have to worry about it anymore? It wasn't Dr. Jordan who had logged on to my comp-board. He didn't have any access to a computer in his prison bunk. No. He'd been cabled to the wall just like Blaine Steven. Any access that Dr. Jordan did have could only have happened during the midnight-to-early-morning hours when he was out of his bunk, as shown by the computer's activity log of the hatch openings to his prison bunk.

Someone else on this ship had helped him get in and out of his bunk. Was that person still on the ship?

No, I decided, definitely not. Because the computer had slammed shut all the hatches, trapping everyone in their bunks. And because the computer had programmed the engine and communications system to make sure everyone remaining on the ship would die sooner or later. Whoever had helped Dr. Jordan would do his or her best not to be on the ship when the escape pod ejected.

But the only person off the ship right now with Dr. Jordan was Luke Daab.

In all that had happened since their escape, none of us had questioned why Dr. Jordan had taken a hostage with him. That was one extra person to use food and water on the escape pod. Dr. Jordan didn't need a hostage if everyone left behind on the ship was going to die anyway. Unless Luke wasn't a hostage.

Luke Daab. The same Luke Daab who had made it possible for Dr. Jordan to ask Ashley about her escape from the Hammerhead space torpedo?

Now I knew why Dr. Jordan had wanted to know. To make sure Ashley didn't have some unexpected way of getting out of the *Moon Racer*. Or some unexpected way of rescuing us.

But Luke Daab?

Images flashed into my mind. Luke in the computer room, with wall panels out and wiring exposed. Luke in the corridor, with ceiling panels out and wiring exposed. Luke working wherever he wanted on the ship, almost invisible to people who passed by him.

A maintenance engineer could come and go anywhere on the ship without ever being questioned. Just like a maintenance engineer could come and go anywhere under the dome without ever being questioned. The same maintenance engineer who had been under the Mars Dome since it had been first established.

Luke Daab?

Another image flashed into my mind. Of Luke shouting something as Ashley and Dad and I had rushed down the corridor and first met them about to enter the escape pod. Something we couldn't hear above the noise of the wailing siren. I had assumed he was shouting to us. What if he had been shouting to Dr. Jordan?

If Luke was the mastermind behind all of this, maybe he was commanding Dr. Jordan to make it look like a hostage situation. Commanding Dr. Jordan to put a choke hold on him and fool us.

But why? If Luke had set it up so that we were all going to die anyhow, why would he want us to think he was a helpless victim? So Dad wouldn't shoot them with the neuron gun? No. The mainframe had already been programmed to shut the neuron gun down. Luke and Dr. Jordan knew that. They weren't afraid of the neuron gun.

So we wouldn't tackle them? No, by the time we got there, they were close enough to jump into the escape pod before we could close the gap.

Then why go to the pretense of making it look like a hostage situation?

When the answer hit me, I shouted out loud.

Then raced to find Dad.

CHAPTER 23

"Here! I found it!"

Dad's voice rang inside the walls of Luke Daab's bunk.

There were three of us. Dad. Ashley. Me. All of us pulling away wall and ceiling panels to find what Luke might have hidden.

Until now, we only had his personal comp-board, which he had left behind the netting of a storage shelf. But a comp-board had nowhere near the power needed to crunch out the code needed to override the mainframe. Which was what I had guessed only 10 minutes earlier while keyboarding my latest journal entry.

"And it's got an infrared antenna." Dad pointed to a small computer hard drive nestled into a compartment behind a wall panel. "So he could not only link wireless to the mainframe but also to his comp-board. It's the go-between computer. It could intercept anything—even Rawling's *real* e-mails to you. You were right, Tyce. If Luke decided not to take this with him, he sure wouldn't want us finding it. With any luck, Lance can use this hard drive to regain control of the mainframe."

"Yes and no," Lance reported to Dad a half hour later. Ashley and I had waited in the navigation cone with Dad, each of us hardly speaking because of the nervous tension.

"Yes, I've regained control of the mainframe," Lance continued. "And, no, the communications system is totally disabled. As are the controls to the flaps and reverse thruster."

"But if you've got the mainframe back . . ."

Lance laughed sourly. "The guy's a genius. And very, very cautious. As if he anticipated the one-in-a-thousand chance we'd find his computer setup in his bunk. He programmed the mainframe alarm system to be silenced so it would seem like everything on board the ship was normal. But it isn't."

"I don't like the sound of this," Dad said.

"You shouldn't," Lance answered. "Luke Daab wrecked the communications systems and piloting controls the old-fashioned way. With a hammer."

"With a hammer!" It was as if Lance had slapped Dad's face.

Lance nodded. "He was the maintenance engineer. Always carried his tool belt. Had the perfect excuse to be wherever he wanted on the ship. Sometime in the last day or two he took a hammer to the physical components of the systems. Just like he destroyed all the vital computer parts of the second escape pod to make sure we couldn't eject it if somehow we regained control of the mainframe. Normally the mainframe would clang out alarm bells louder than a fire alarm as soon as it detected the malfunction. But with the computer programmed to ignore the malfunction signals . . ."

"We've got nothing, then. We're stuck on a ship with no communications and no manual piloting controls."

"All I was able to do was reduce the burn rate of our fuel to nothing, for now. We've stopped accelerating. Even so, if we don't figure out a way to start slowing down in the next hour, we'll shoot too far past Earth for our emergency beacon to reach anyone."

"So if we are somehow able to start slowing down right away," Ashley said, "someone might come looking?"

"If we stop." Dad swung in his chair to face her squarely. "And if we stop close enough to the orbital shipping lanes between Earth and Mars. Neither possibility gives us much hope."

I hadn't spoken since Lance had entered the navigation cone. "There is," I said, "one tiny chance."

Everyone stared at me.

"Hey," I finished, "the big bots are still in the cargo bay, aren't they?"

CHAPTER 24

Darkness.

Since I wasn't receiving the light signals through human eyes, waiting wasn't going to help my vision adjust. But that didn't matter. I knew that within moments light from the stars and sun would flood the inside of the cargo bay.

I heard a muted clank as the lock released. Then a hiss as the vacuum of outer space sucked the air out of the cargo bay. That was the last sound I could expect to hear. Sound does not travel in a vacuum, and the cargo bay slowly swung open to expose my robot body to the open solar system.

Light entered. The light of millions of galaxies and billions of stars, so diamond clear that I felt a thrill of incredible joy.

There was movement beside me. The other robot,

controlled by Ashley. Like me, she was hooked by remote to a computer hard drive in the robot center inside the *Moon Racer*.

The robot waved. I waved back.

She had a newer model, but both were constructed with similar designs.

The lower body of the robot is much like my wheelchair. Instead of a pair of legs, an axle connects two wheels. On land, just like a wheelchair, it turns by moving one wheel forward while the other wheel remains motionless or moves backward.

The robot's upper body is a short, thick, hollow pole that sticks through the axle, with a heavy weight to counterbalance the arms and head. Within this weight is the battery that powers the robot, with wires running up inside the hollow pole.

At the upper end of the pole is a crosspiece to which arms are attached. The arms swing freely without hitting the wheels. Like the rest of the robot, they are made of titanium and are jointed like human arms, with one difference. All the joints swivel. The hands, too, are like human hands, but with only three fingers and a thumb instead of four fingers and a thumb.

Four video lenses at the top of the pole serve as eyes. One faces forward, one backward, and one to each side.

Three tiny microphones, attached to the underside of the video lenses, play the role of ears, taking in sound. The fourth speaker, underneath the video lens that faces forward, produces sound and allows us to make our voices heard.

The computer drive is well protected within the hollow titanium pole that serves as the robot's upper body. Since it's mounted on shock absorbers, the robot can fall 10 feet without shaking the computer drive. This computer drive has a short antenna plug at the back of the pole to send and receive X-ray signals.

Both of our robots held handjets in their right hands to allow us to propel the robots through space. My own robot held a welder's torch in the left hand. Ashley's robot held eight narrow strips of metal, all of them about two feet long. Everything had been placed in the cargo bay before Ashley and I had started the control sequence.

I waved one more time, then pointed at the open cargo door.

Her robot waved back and nodded.

I pushed forward. We had work to do.

The cargo bay had an inner door, which sealed the *Moon Racer* from outer space while the outer door was open. For humans who had to return to the inside of the *Moon Racer*, this was important. On their return from space the outer door would be closed and sealed, then the inner door opened, allowing air back into the cargo bay. Without the outer door closed again, it would be suicide for everyone in the *Moon Racer* to open the inner door.

For robots, however, it didn't matter. Not if they didn't ever need to get inside the *Moon Racer*. That simple fact was the only chance of survival for everyone else.

Because what we had to do would mean destroying the outer wide, flat cargo door.

I hit a propellant button on my handjet and pushed toward the cargo door.

Ashley followed. Each robot was attached to the wall of the cargo bay by hundreds of yards of thin cable that would prevent it from being lost in space.

Near the hinges of the cargo door, I stopped. I was now half inside the cargo bay and half outside, with the door wide open. I looked down at my wheels. Below, nothingness stretched to infinity.

It was not the time to enjoy a view, however. I clicked the button that fired up the welder's torch.

Ashley and I had gone over this a dozen times inside the spaceship. She knew what her robot had to do. I knew my robot's job. I nodded one more time to let her know I was ready.

She tucked her own handjet under the robot arm so both hands were free.

My handjet was off, and I used it to tap a spot on the edge of the door near the lower hinge.

Immediately Ashley's robot placed the end of one of the metal strips against the spot I had touched. Her robot held it there while I welded it on. The weld cooled almost instantly in the black chill of space. I handed her robot the torch and bent the strip upward, then back down, so it formed an upside-down U. I took the torch from her robot and welded the other end of the strip in place. We had formed our first bracket.

We did it again, a little higher. The two brackets were now a shoulder width apart.

Then we moved outward, staying with the door. At the opposite end of the door, near the latch that would hold it in place when it was shut, my robot body hung motionless, with infinity stretching in every direction.

But it was still no time to enjoy the view. Or even to marvel at the fact that we clung to a spaceship moving at thousands upon thousands of miles per hour, but without air around us, we didn't seem to be moving at all.

On this end of the door, I welded one bracket, then another. These two were also a shoulder width apart, roughly parallel with the two on the other side. Now we had four primitive handholds permanently attached to the inner side of the door.

Aware of how important it was to move quickly, I pointed at the last two brackets. Ashley's robot nodded and handed me the remaining four strips of metal. I bent them in a rough circle around the edge of one of my robot wheels. I nodded.

Her robot grabbed a bracket in each hand and hung there from the outer edge of the door, as if hanging from a handhold in the corridor of the *Moon Racer*. Her robot remained there while I used my handjet to move back to the hinges. Without hesitation, using the incredible heat of the welding torch in my other hand, I cut the hinges loose. The door fell away from the *Moon Racer*.

With Ashley's robot still hanging from the brackets, I guided the door through the weightlessness of outer space, back toward the ion thruster of the *Moon Racer*.

We were halfway done.

The ion thruster was simply a giant nozzle that directed a stream of propelling ions into space. If Lance had not been able to turn down the fuel-burn ratio earlier, our plan would not have had a chance.

As it was, it would still be tricky.

When we arrived, I used my handjet to push the wheels of Ashley's robot against the outer wall of the giant nozzle. I took one of the strips of metal I'd wrapped around my own robot wheels and bent it into another U. I turned the U upside down and put it between the spokes of one of her robot wheels. I welded one end to the outer wall of the thruster, then the other. I had just bracketed her robot per- manently into place. I did the same with her other wheel.

All of this happened in slow-motion ballet. Movements in outer space have to be smooth and even, something I had learned the hard way during virtual-reality sessions. I wished it could go faster, but I had to get it right the first time.

It did look strange.

Her robot was now attached by its wheels to the outside of the thruster nozzle. And its hands held the brackets I had welded on the cargo door.

Three-quarters of the way there.

I left Ashley's robot there and pushed around to the opposite side of the ion thruster. With the final two strips of metal, I welded U-shaped strips around my own wheels so that my robot, too, was permanently attached to the outside of the thruster nozzle.

I waved at Ashley's robot on the other side of the nozzle. It was weird, thinking that each of these robot bodies moved because of the brain-wave impulses that Ashley and I were sending to computers inside the *Moon Racer*. And weird to think that very soon Ashley and I would wake up inside the robot lab, with these two robots remaining out here, doing a highly unexpected job. *If* my plan worked.

I nodded one final time and watched as her robot began to swing the door down toward the opening of the thruster. Had there been ions streaming out, it would have blown the door backward like a flap in the wind. Instead, her robot was able to lower the door until my robot could grab the handhold brackets on the opposite side.

Just like that, we were finished.

Now there was a robot on each side, holding the door like an umbrella, just a few feet above the nozzle of the ion thruster.

CHAPTER 25

"Ready?" Dad asked Lance.

"As ready as we'll ever be," he replied.

Ashley and I crowded behind Dad as he watched the monitor with Lance. Everyone else was in the entertainment cluster, waiting just as anxiously as we were.

"Then fire it up," Dad said. "We need to start as soon as possible. My calculations show we'll barely make it as it is."

If it works, I thought.

Lance rapidly keyed some commands.

For several seconds, nothing happened.

"Is the fuel-burn ratio up?" Dad asked.

Lance pointed at the computer screen. "That's what it says. But it always takes a bit of time for the ions to—"

Bang!

The *Moon Racer* lurched, throwing us to the side.

All of us hit the opposite wall as the *Moon Racer* suddenly slowed.

And we began to cheer! More cheers reached us from the corridor. The others, too, understood we had just felt sudden deceleration.

It had worked.

The cargo door was now funneling the ions in the same way that a reverse thruster would!

Dad hugged me. I hugged Ashley. Lance hugged all three of us.

"Okay," Dad said. "Lance, monitor it closely. But thanks to Tyce and Ashley's quick work to help us slow down and the fuel we have left, we should get this thing almost to a standstill by the time we reach Earth. And with the emergency locator, someone will find us soon enough."

Lance's big grin faded.

"I know. I know," Dad said. "Then you'll face arrest when we get Earth-side. But with all that you've done now and if you testify against Dr. Jordan and Luke Daab, I don't think it will be as bad as you expect. And I'll do whatever I can to help."

Trouble was, almost three weeks later, when the soldiers of a military rescue shuttle boarded the ship, the first people arrested were Dad and me.

CHAPTER 26

03.27.2040

Of all my dreams about Earth, I never expected I would get here and not see anything except four walls of a prison cell. I now know the true definition of misery. My body aches. After a lifetime of gravity at only one-third of the planet Earth's, my bones feel heavy, my muscles weak, and my lungs tired. At every point where my body sits in my wheelchair, my skin is raw from the unaccustomed weight and pressure. I can't imagine how much worse this would have been if I hadn't been working out daily during the trip from Mars to Earth.

Dad said it would take a week at least to adjust to the new gravity, but I wonder if I ever will.

As for my dreams about all the different foods I'd be able to try, those too have become a nightmare. Prison food is horrible.

I don't know exactly where I am, just that it's some windowless room the size of a closet, and it has been two days since our arrest.

I haven't seen my dad. Or Ashley. And I'm not sure what happened to them or the others because we were arrested so quickly. All I have is my compboard, and even its files were searched, copied, and transferred before I could keep it.

So now I'm writing my journal in case Dad or Mom or Rawling ever gets ahold of this.

All I can do is hope. . . .

I stopped keyboarding at the sound of scratching on my prison door. It sounded like the guard's keys. Which meant I would get yet another rotten meal.

It wasn't a guard. But a robot!

"Hello," a familiar voice said from the robot's speakers. "You all right, Tyce?"

"Ashley? Ashley!" I pushed forward, expecting that I would float through the air in her direction. Nothing happened. I was on Earth, not in the freedom and weightlessness of space.

"Shhh!" she said anxiously. "We only have about five minutes."

"For what?" I asked.

"What else?" she said. "Escape. You and I have a lot to do before all of this is over."

SCIENCE AND GOD

You've probably noticed that the question of God's existence comes up in Robot Wars.

It's no accident, of course. I think this is one of the most important questions that we need to decide for ourselves. If God created the universe and there is more to life than what we can see, hear, taste, smell, or touch, that means we have to think of our own lives as more than just the time we spend on Earth.

On the other hand, if this universe was not created and God does not exist, then that might really change how you view your existence and how you live.

Sometimes science is presented in such a way that it suggests there is no God. To make any decision, it helps to know as much about the situation as possible. As you decide for yourself, I'd like to show in the Robot Wars series that many, many people—including famous scientists—don't see science this way.

As you might guess, I've spent a lot of time wondering about science and God, and I've spent a lot of time reading about what scientists have learned and concluded. Because of this, I wrote a nonfiction book called *Who Made The Moon?* and you can find information about it at www.whomadethemoon.com. If you ever read it, you'll see why science does not need to keep anyone away from God.

With that in mind, I've added a little bit more to this book—a couple of essays about the science in journals one and two of Robot Wars, based on what you can find in *Who Made The Moon?*

Sigmund Brouwer
whomadethemoon.com

JOURNAL ONE
DOES GOD SPEAK TO PEOPLE?

Q: *Does God speak to people?*

A: I believe yes.

Perhaps not with an actual voice. But through our conscience, through quiet moments when we suddenly understand something that wasn't clear before, through the gentle instruction from other people who know him well.

But what many people struggle with is that the ways God speaks to us often can't be proven. As Tyce learns in this book, having faith in God means you decide to trust him, even when you can't see the outcome. Since scientists are used to seeing results and proof, and since it's scientifically impossible to prove God exists, some of them want to think the only things that exist are the things you can measure.

Why do so many scientists see a conflict between science (data that can be proven by A + B = C) and faith (something you feel inside your heart and believe with your mind but can't hear, taste, or touch)? It's true that believing in God means taking a leap of faith. But believing in God isn't totally illogical, as some people believe.

You see, humans are not just made of body and mind. We are capable of love. Of loneliness. Of longing. Things that can't be measured or found during a medical examination. Things that also point to the existence of a soul.

When God speaks to us, I believe he speaks to our souls.

As Tyce realized in this book, we just have to find those quiet moments where we can hear him. We have to learn to listen.

JOURNAL TWO
WILL COMPUTERS SOMEDAY REPLACE MAN?

Q: Are computers smarter than people?

A: Computers already surround us. And in the future, they'll become even more important. Just look at Tyce Sanders's world, where Lance Evenson, the chief computer technician, is the most important person on the Moon Racer! After all, he's the guy who keeps the computers running on this intergalactic 2040 spaceship.

But you know what? This mission shows that all the technology in the world can't match our human ingenuity. When the computer system is useless, Tyce's creativity—using the robots to slow down the Moon Racer—is what saves the spaceship from shooting past Earth into deep, black nothingness. Tyce's dad's quick, instinctive reactions keep the hatch door from locking them in. And Tyce even has to "rescue" the ant-bot by knotting threads from a regulation jumpsuit to fish the robot out of the air vent. I guess robots aren't so smart after all!

Q: Why does God want us to make good decisions?

A: Humans created robots and computers, and that's why they have problems. It's because we humans aren't perfect, either. Although we are created by God, in his image, he gives us a choice: Will we follow him and his ways or not?

Some people, like Blaine Steven, count on technology and power to get what they want. But such things can't save them from possible death. When ex-director Steven thought he might die, all of a sudden he began to ask Tyce questions about faith and God. Tyce was shocked, because Steven seemed like somebody who'd never want to know—or care—about religion.

But appearances can be deceiving. Tyce found that out the hard way. He had accused Lance Evenson, who looked like a tough guy, of being the mastermind behind the plot. When the whole time it was actually weak and drab Luke Daab who fooled them all.

We humans look at appearances, but God looks at the heart. Because God loves us, he encourages us to make right decisions. Why? Because he knows bad decisions can affect us for a lifetime and he hurts when we hurt. He also knows that such a lifestyle drives us away from him.

Q: Can you ever do something so wrong that God will never take you back?

A: Now that my wife, Cindy, and I have two daughters, Olivia and Savannah, I understand even more fully the promises that God made to us as humans. No matter what lifestyle decisions our daughters might ever make down the road, no matter how far away from us they might go, all they would have to do is turn around and reach out for us, and we would take them back with joy.

The same is true with God and his love for us. No matter how far we might stray from him, he is always waiting with love and hope for our return. (Just read the parable of the Prodigal Son for proof!)

When Jesus walked this world, he had an incredible message. You see, the religious leaders of his time taught that in order to approach God and be with him, you had to first make yourself right by paying penalties for what you had done wrong. Jesus said it was the opposite. All you need to do is approach God through his Son, Jesus, admit your wrongs, and ask for forgiveness. Then God will enter your life and transform it, giving you hope, peace, and joy for the future. Then, when life on this Earth is over, you'll find your real home. In heaven. In God's love.

And that's something only humans can experience—not computers.

ABOUT THE AUTHOR

Sigmund Brouwer and his wife, recording artist Cindy
Morgan, and their daughters split living between Red Deer,
Alberta, Canada, and Nashville, Tennessee. He has written
several series of juvenile fiction and eight novels. Sigmund
loves sports and plays golf and hockey. He also enjoys visit-
ing schools to talk about books. He welcomes visitors to his
Web site at www.coolreading.com.

Tim Carhardt is drifting through life with one goal—survival. Jamie Maxwell believes she can become—no, *will* become—the first female winner of the cup. But life isn't always as easy as it seems. What happens when dreams and faith hit the wall?

#1 *Blind Spot*
#2 *Over the Wall*
#3 *Overdrive*
#4 *Checkered Flag*

The four-book RPM series spans a year of the chase for the cup. Each story is filled with fast-paced races as well as fast-paced adventure off the track.

All four books available now!

CP0206